CAUTION IN LOVE

PART 1

CAUTION IN LOVE

K. RODRIGUEZ

AUTHOR'S NOTE

Caution in Love is Part One of Izzy and Chase's story and ends in a happily-for-now. Their love story continues in _Worth the Risk_—where everything they've been building toward finally leads to their HEA.

Content warning: Caution in love is a romance novella with open door intimate scenes, explicit language, no cliffhanger and a happily-for-now ending. Trigger warnings include alcoholism and verbal abuse from a parent, mentions of childhood neglect, miscommunication trope, mentions of cheating (not any of the MCs). **If any of these themes trigger you, please do no read.**

PLAYLIST

1.Karma by Queen Naiji

2. Amargura by Karol G

3. Te Olvido by Manuel Turizo

4.Real Thing by Ruel

5. Me Fijé by Alex Rose and Rauw Alejandro

6. Wonder by Shawn Mendes

7. Evergreen by Mt. Joy

8. My Stress by NF

9. Niña Bonita by Fred and Sean Paul

10. Thinking Bout You by Frank Ocean

11. Feels Right by Alina Baraz

12. Let it Hurt by Daniel Saint Black

13. Take it Home by Alina Baraz

14. I Don't Want To Lose You by Luca Fogale

15. I'm Ready by Sam Smith and Demi Lovato

16. Like I Want You by Giveon

17. Forever My Love by J Balvin and Ed Sheehan

CAUTION in Love

Caribbean Spanish to English
terms & translations

Ese cara de culo - That ass face
mama guevo - motherf**er
párate - stand up
Ahora si - That's right
Mira, mira - Look, look
Nena - babygirl
No comience - Don't start
Chismosa - nosey
que lindo - how nice
Buenas, buenas, mi gente - Hello, hello, my people
Oye - Hey!
Carajo - Dammit
chancleta - flip-flop
sucia - nasty
callate, muchacha - shut up, girl!

Of all forms of caution, **caution in love** is perhaps the most fatal to true happiness.

— BERTRAND RUSSELL

1

IZZY

"*S*top the car, and back the fuck up. *Ese cara de culo* did not break up with you in a text!"

My best friend Mya's voice blares through my car's speakers, drowning out the sound of the torrential rain outside while my mind replays said text message currently in question. My hands tighten their grip on the steering wheel. It is taking every ounce of dwindling self-control I have left to not turn this car around and give that pathetic excuse of a man-child a real piece of my mind.

"What a little bitch. I swear, I hate him so much! Stupid-ass cheating *mama guevo!*" she continues shouting as if Esteban can hear her from our Philly apartment—correction: now *his* Philly apartment. I groan out loud at that last thought.

I remember the day he signed that lease, reassuring me that the shitty credit he left me with—while perfecting his own score—was the only reason. It was evident even then that he never planned for me to be in his future.

I slam my foot on the accelerator and drive through yet another yellow light just as it turns red. I should be driving

I

more carefully on these slick wet roads. It's been raining all day, and everyone on this side of the river knows it doesn't take much for the Schuylkill to overflow and flood the neighboring streets.

"Ooooh, he is lucky I am carrying this child right now, or I swear he'd be catching these hands!"

The image my mind conjures does put a small smile on my face as I picture Mya now, rolling up her sleeves, removing her earrings, huffing and puffing and tying her hair up in a bun over her head.

She is loyal to a mother-effing T, and I don't deserve any of it because the truth is I have been a pitiful friend to her.

Yup, I'm that friend. The one who puts all her time and energy into her boyfriend while neglecting everyone else in her life.

Worst of all, she is entering her final month of pregnancy, and although I should be happy for her—I mean, I am happy for her—I just can't help myself from envying her. Of course, I will never tell her that, but damnit, Mya was always the wild child. Miss Single and Happy as a Pringle. She never even wanted marriage, let alone kids. She would constantly tease me for my own—as she called them—Disney-like dreams.

But here she is, my beautiful best friend, absolutely glowing and truly the happiest I have ever seen her—swept off her feet, married, and starting the family she swore she would never want.

I can't help but feel like, for just a second, she's living my life. The life I've always wanted—secure, stable, and not at all as batshit crazy as the life I had growing up.

"Fuck him. He isn't shit without you, Izzy," Mya adds, interrupting me from my thoughts.

Tears form in my eyes, blurring the already fuzzy road in front of me.

"I know." My throat squeezes into a tight knot. The emotions I've been trying to keep at bay, at least for the duration of this car ride, threaten to break free.

Don't you do it, Izzy. We are not wasting another goddamn tear on him.

"Are you okay?" she asks, her voice growing soft.

I nod my head, trying to convince myself I'm fine, but my mouth, of course, betrays me.

"No," my voice wavers.

Big, fat tears fall down my cheeks as the dam holding them back finally gives out.

"I'm so stupid! I really thought he was going to propose!" I cry out, slamming my hand against the steering wheel. "I spent my entire last paycheck on fucking lingerie and a dress I can barely breathe in for a special anniversary night. And then...and then"—I hiccup and take a lungful of air—"I waited for two hours, calling and texting, worried something had happened to him. Mya, I was two seconds away from calling the hospital when I got a selfie of some half-naked girl barely covered in a bedsheet, and behind her, that goddamn motherfucker was pulling his pants on." That stupid tattoo of his, stretched across his shoulder blades, mocked me through the goddamn screen.

Solo Dios me puedes juzgar.

As if that's all the pardon he needs to get away with what-ever he wants in life.

"But that's not even the worst part." *Because what could possibly be worse than finding out that the man you were expecting a ring from is actually a cheating asshole?* "I wanted him to deny it so bad, Mya." I gasp as the words tumble out, echoing in the small space around me. I hate myself so much for being *that woman*. The one who pushes everyone away and is even willing to push her own self-worth down the drain, all for a man. If I learned anything from my mother and the countless men that she paraded in and right back out the door when they acted up, it is to NOT be that woman.

"I'm so sorry, Izzy-boo."

"He didn't even care. Literally, an *"Oh shit"* text a minute later. And that was it. That was all he had to say about it. So, I packed my shit and left." I keep to myself how I called him and begged him for more of an explanation. How if he had apologized and groveled just a little bit, I would have forgiven him and tried my best to move on with our life together. *Damn it, no!*

I wipe my cheeks with the back of my hand and take in a shallow, ragged breath.

"Come over," Mya says. "We can have a girls' night like we used to. Kev can make us snacks and pick up some pizza."

The idea of Mya's sweet husband catering to us all night long does sound way better than the pity party I have planned for myself, but with being less than a minute from my mom's house, I just want to put this all behind me and be done with this night.

"Tomorrow, I promise. I'm almost at Mom's, and I just really want to sleep," I say as I turn right onto her street. The rain has finally let up a bit, and I can finally make out the parts of the neighborhood I grew up in. The street is lined with the same two-story red-brick row homes, tall oak trees take up far too much space on the narrow sidewalks, and the two pillars of the community, Ms. Dee's daycare center and Sammy's Bodega, sit on the corner.

"You know you won't be getting any sleep over there. Your sister doesn't put those monsters to bed until they crash. Where are you even supposed to sleep, anyway?"

She has a point. My mother's house has been at full capacity since...well, always, but still. There is no way I can impose on Mya and Kev right now, especially as they are hopefully days away from expecting their first baby.

"I just got to Mom's, but soon, I promise," I say as I bite down on my bottom lip, holding back the sob that wants to break free.

"Fine. At least now I don't have to commute all the way into the city to see you anymore. We have to make up for lost time before this baby gets here," she says excitedly as the pit in my stomach squeezes tight.

"Tell Kev I said hi, and give extra belly rubs to my peanut," I say as I pull into a parking spot.

"Yes, Aunty Izzy. Love you."

"Love you back."

I end the call and let my head fall against the steering wheel.

I am not ready for this.

It's one thing to come back and visit from time to time, but I haven't actually lived here since college, and thank God that was just for holidays and a few weeks in the summer, then I met Esteban my second year at Penn. Of course, breaks in the Dominican Republic, where his parents still lived, sounded way more appealing than Norristown, Pennsylvania. Before I knew it, I was only dropping in when someone needed something.

I'd never left the country, let alone flown in an airplane, before I met him. So many firsts I'd given him, thinking it meant something.

Thinking I meant something.

If I had known what I know right now, I wouldn't have given in so quickly, so easily, so goddamn naively.

Who am I kidding? One look into those soulful brown eyes of his, and I practically reached into my chest, tore my heart out, and put it in his hands to do with as he pleased.

Now look at me. Twenty-six-years old, brokenhearted, and Betty, my old and trusty Toyota Prius, is filled with the last five years of my life in garbage bags.

My life is now basically trash, and the real kicker is moving back home. Back to sharing one bathroom with at least eight other people and the chaos home has always been.

How fun.

It's okay. I'll be okay. This is temporary. I can survive a whole life here, so what's a few months—just until I can save up and get my own place. Though, with my poor excuse of an income, it'll probably be some tiny studio in Fishtown. Nothing at all like the Park Place condo Esteban will have all to himself now.

I take one more deep breath before shutting the car off and grab a bag from the backseat before trudging slowly up the steps. The TV on the other side of the door is playing so loud I can feel its vibrations through the porch floor, along with screaming I know for a fact is coming from my sister's badass kids.

There's no place like home, right?

2

IZZY

"*I*sadora Leticia, get your ass up!"

My mother's voice tears me from my slumber.

"Five more minutes," I beg, even though I know it is only going to get the sheets pulled right off me. I clamp my fingers around the thin fabric, squeezing my eyes shut, and hold on for dear life as I listen to the steady drum of her feet stomping toward me. And just as I expected, in one quick motion, the blanket is torn from my body. My legs curl up into the fetal position in an attempt to keep warm.

"Why is it so cold in this house?" I cry out, tucking my arms out of the sleeves of my sweatshirt and wrapping them around my chest.

"Did you forget to pay the bill again?" I open one eye to watch her reaction.

"Excuse me, but that was one time."

"Two," I correct her.

"Girl, so help me God."

It's been seven months since my return to the hell I grew up in.

Okay, okay, I'm being dramatic. Not quite hell, but as you can see, there is no peace here. Or privacy. God, I miss having my own space—four walls and a door I can call my own. I would gladly take a cupboard under the stairs over my mother's stiff-as-a-board, mid-century, vintage sofa complete with plastic and vinyl covering.

"Now, get up. My poor mother is rolling around in her grave, watching you live on her couch like this."

I groan and search my body for at least a semblance of energy to crawl out of this cocoon just so I can get away from my mother and her nagging right now.

"Leave Mamá out of this." I sit up and cringe at the bright light seeping in through the windows and into the narrow living/dining room, also known as my current bedroom. A blend of new and old-school Dominican, thanks to Mamá Ingrid. She passed away ten years ago and left it all to Mom, who, of course, kept every single thing—the furniture, the clothes, even the vintage Pyrex collection.

"Early? Princessa, it is well past noon. Now, párate. My living room looks like a pigsty, and Luis is coming over later," she says, folding my blanket and rushing me up off the couch.

Reluctantly, I drag myself out of bed, exhaling a deep sigh and groaning in the process. "I'm going."

Before I'm even up the stairs, I hear Aiden and Alfonso, my nephews, charging down the hallway.

"Finally! We been waiting all day to play," Aiden says as he brushes past me down the stairs and straight to the Xbox in the living room.

"Old people sleep so much," his little brother, Alfonso, adds.

Little shits.

The level of disrespect in kids these days is ridiculous. I would have never even thought about talking to an adult that way at seven years old. I see it all day, every day as a second-grade teacher, and honestly, some days it makes me question my profession.

When I reach the bathroom, the sight in the mirror makes me jump back—though, I mean, by now I really should be used to such a pitiful reflection. My red-rimmed eyes are puffy from yet another restless night, which only makes my deep-set eyes more prominent. My dark, wavy hair I had tied up in a knot at the top of my head before bed hangs crooked on one side instead. And then there's the glob of pizza sauce glued to my chin.

One look at me like this, and you wouldn't think I spent the week prior as a fully functioning human, molding young minds, and changing the world one student at a time, would you?

No.

I look homeless.

Shit. I am homeless.

"Hurry up in there!"

My head falls back at the sound of my older sister, Leslie, pounding her fist on the other side of the bathroom door. I swear her bladder is connected to this door swinging shut, because every damn day, as soon as I close the door behind me, not a second passes that she isn't on that other side, rushing me out. I know her conniving ass does it on purpose.

Deciding to ignore her, I carry on with the rest of my morning routine, taking my sweet-ass time. I brush my teeth, cleanse and moisturize my face, comb my hair, and then let the water run for another few minutes just because. Her incessant banging on the door nearly knocks the shampoo and conditioner off the shelf. *Fuck you, Leslie.*

Eventually, I decide to unlock the door, but as soon as I press the button on the knob to unlock it, Leslie barges in, leaving the door wide open and not wasting any time rolling her pants down before plopping onto the toilet.

"You've turned into a real bitch, Izzy!" she hollers.

"Takes one to know one," I say as I slam the door shut, smiling and feeling very pleased with myself and my childish antics. She is right. I have been a little bitchier than my usual self since being back home.

Oh well. You know where being nice has gotten me? Nowhere but right back where I started.

Down the stairs, I pass my nephews already heavily engrossed in some combat game I'm pretty sure they are way too young for. The TV screen slows down on a character getting their throat sliced. The graphics make it look so damn real that I have to look away. *Nope. No, no, no. I will not think of my nephews as little psychopaths.*

Though, I am slightly concerned they will turn into ones with games like these.

I turn away and reach for the remote on the couch and then shut the TV off as I play dumb and head straight for the Keurig.

"Hey!" they both cry out in unison. *Muahahaha.*

"So, what are your plans for the day?" Mom asks in that tone that tells me she knows damn well what my plans are. They have been the same every weekend since I have been back home.

Sleep in, coffee up, order Grubhub, and cyber-stalk Esteban's and his new girlfriend's social media accounts until Monday morning.

If I wasn't at an all-time low, I would be disgusted with myself.

I pop a Café Bustelo into the K-cup holder.

"Same as usual, Ma," I say as my mouth instantly begins to salivate over the rich aroma sure to fill my mug.

"Well, Liam is with his father today, and the twins have volleyball."

"Okay," I say, unconcerned by my other siblings' schedule for the day. I will miss my little Liam. He's my favorite little brother—and not just because he is my only brother.

"Leslie and I are headed to the gym. You should come with us."

I gag at the thought as I add creamer to my mug and stir.

"The wedding is eight weeks away now, and you agreed to the membership when I signed you up," she says, pointing a finger in my direction.

I must not do a good job at hiding the grimace that comes across my face, because she immediately purses her lips and cocks her brow in a stern look.

"Obviously I have not been in the right state of mind, Mother."

Leslie strides into the kitchen, brushing past me, "You haven't been in the right state of mind because you spend all your weekends holed up on that couch, clinging to that raggedy old sweatshirt." She pinches the arm of my sweatshirt and contorts her face before continuing, "Do you even wash it? Please, do us all a favor and put this thing in the trash."

I glare at her and smack her hand off me before giving her my middle finger. She reciprocates without even looking up, sticking a perfectly manicured finger up in my direction.

"You know, your sister has a point. You're never going to move on like this. What have I been telling you?" And because she has been saying it practically every day for the last seven months, Leslie and I repeat what we know, word for word, she will say.

"The best way to get over a man is to get under a new one."

"*Ahora si.* Good to know my girls are listening."

Ladies and gentlemen, my mother.

"Look, it's not for me but for your own mental health, my love. It can be fun, just like back in the day. You remember, before the other three, it was us three," Mom says, wrapping her arms around me. "And who knows, if some man is lucky enough to catch your eye, maybe he will whisk you away, and the next wedding we plan will be yours."

Her words make my heart squeeze tight in my chest.

A year ago, I really thought it would be my wedding I'd be planning by now. Instead, I'm here helping her plan her third.

"But if she isn't coming, she can watch the boys. Looks like Jimmy is a no-show," Leslie says, glaring down at her phone.

"Again?" Mom takes a step back, and all three of us shake our heads together.

Fucking Jimmy—Leslie's deadbeat ex and poor excuse for a father to my nephews. It sucks that he bailed on the boys again, but it will be a cold day in hell when I babysit those heathens.

"Hell no. The bruising on my ass has still not healed from the last time you left me with them."

"Oh my God, why are you so dramatic? There is no way you're bruised."

"When your ass gets blasted by a fully automatic Nerf gun for one hundred rounds, then you can tell me that shit doesn't hurt."

"See, this is why you need to come with us to the gym," Mom cuts in, turning around and smacking her hand against her butt. "Get you some glutes of steel like your momma!"

Lord, you really outdid yourself when you created her, didn't you?

"*Mira, mira.*" She flexes her ass cheeks, making them jump up.

"Okay, okay! I'll go, just please stop!" I beg, covering my face with my hands. Speaking of leaving the house... "Is Jimmy done with my car yet, Leslie?"

Betty in her prime was the safest, most reliable car in the market. Any problems I ever had were minor things that needed replacing, but, of course, when it rains it fucking pours. I was supposed to be saving up for my own place, but instead, I've been dumping every one of my paychecks into repairs.

"Do I look like a mechanic? I don't know shit about your car. Call the garage if you need an update."

"You're the one that pressed me into taking the car to his shop!" I shout.

"Ay! Stop fighting! Grown-ass women still bickering like children. Leslie call Jimmy, and you go get dressed."

I turn around and walk out to the hallway closet where I have been storing some of my things. I rummage through the plastic bins housing my wardrobe and pull out a pair of relaxed black sweatpants and an oversized crop top.

I try to avoid my reflection in the mirror hanging on the back of the closet door. One sad look is enough, but my eyes catch onto the frayed sweatshirt I've been clinging to for months.

I hate the person in the mirror so much. I hate that I let myself become this pathetic, this level of pitiful, for a man I know never deserved me, never valued me, and probably never even loved me.

"Not anymore," I mutter to myself as I rip the sweatshirt off over my head.

The best way to get over a man is to get the fuck over it.

3

———

IZZY

The last time I stepped foot in a gym was because it was mandatory to graduate high school. Now, here I am, eight years later and even more insecure than ever, especially walking in with my mom and Leslie in their coordinated leopard-print gym wear. Their outfits highlight every one of their shared assets: perfectly portioned bust and petite hourglass figures—a family trait that, of course, skipped me. Compared to them, I stand out—and not in a good way.

I'll never have a body like theirs. Hell, I'm already jealous of the curves on my little sisters who are barely even sixteen. And Mom, even on her worst days, which are few and far between, can easily pass as Leslie's sister, whereas I look more like a distant relative. Mom's Afro-Latina roots shine through her and every one of my mixed siblings while I managed to turn out as the Latina equivalent of plain fucking Jane. My skin is pale, and instead of getting tan, it very easily burns under the sun. My curves are way more subtle, and any excess weight goes straight to my hips, gut, or arms but not my ass because a girl can't have it all, right?!

"At least you've got a good rack," as Esteban liked to remind me.

Nope. Don't go down that road, Izzy.

As we navigate through the bustling crowd of what looks like amateur bodybuilders and fitness influencers, we come to a stop in front of a row of exercise equipment that most definitely resembles a death trap.

"What the hell is this?" I glare at the contraption in front of me.

"There's a little picture on the side that shows you how to use it," Mom says as she raises her arms over her head, interlocking her fingers and stretching.

"This?" I point. "This is about as useless as Ikea instructions." I let out an exasperated huff and reluctantly slide into the cramped seat, angling myself as the picture indicates. I position my legs on the small foam rollers at the base of the machine and slowly begin to push against them with my feet until Mom interrupts me with a light tap on my shoulder.

"Nena, this is for your arms, not legs. The rollers are just for you to rest your legs on. Here," She reaches in front of me for two arm-shaped handles and guides my hands to grasp them. "You'll pull back here," she instructs.

"Oh," I mutter under my breath, catching Leslie's smirk from the corner of my eye. My cheeks burn red as embarrassment washes over me, and I can't help feeling incredibly self-conscious.

What am I doing here? This is so dumb and-

As if she can hear my thoughts out loud, she says, "You know what? Why don't we skip the equipment for today and try some of the workouts Leslie has been doing, maybe stop at the treadmills, and then call it a day in the sauna."

"Fine, whatever will get this over with sooner." I shimmy myself out of the machine and meet Leslie in front of a padded space with floor-to-ceiling mirrors.

"Okay. The workout is real easy, Izzy. Just a couple of basic moves repeated." She goes on a rant explaining what a HIIT workout stands for, and I'm almost taken aback by her being so interested in something other than herself.

Not ten minutes later...

"I'm..." I wheeze, "...dying!" My hands grip my knees as my body tries to recover from the abuse it is currently enduring.

That earns me a chuckle from Mom and Leslie.

Do the workout, they said. It will be easy, they said.

The only thing getting hit right now is my confidence.

"Just two more, come on. Stop being so dramatic," Leslie calls out, dropping down into a pushup.

"You got this, mama!" Mom cheers, popping up and off the floor effortlessly.

I shake my head, feeling the nausea roll in as small beads of sweat form on my forehead.

"I can't," I say.

I place my hands on my sides and walk around in small circles, appreciating the slight breeze I'm getting from the large overhead fans.

"I'm going to walk," I wheeze, pointing behind myself in the direction of the treadmills we had passed earlier. I turn around and stumble, bumping right into a set of dumbbells. The heavy-set crashes to the floor, just nearly missing my feet.

The sound echoes through the wide space. My ears burn as I feel every other person's eyes piercing into me, and of course Leslie bursts into laughter as Mom rushes to my side to help me replace the dumbbells.

"I was thinking," she says, dropping a dumbbell into its place. "Maybe we should get you set up with a personal trainer. They'll be able to guide you into these workouts better than your sister and—"

"No, Mom. It's fine." It's not that I don't appreciate her concern, because I really do. My whole life, I was always the one she didn't have to worry about—that is until I showed up at her door seven months ago. It's been nothing but, *"Are you okay?"* and *"I'm worried about you"* a hundred times a day.

"I'm just worried about you," she says, which instantly makes my eyes roll back into my head. The look in her eyes, though, makes my stomach curl. I look away, and I drop the last weight into its place.

"I'm okay, Mom," I say a little too forced and head as far away from her and Leslie as possible.

I make my way to the other side of the gym, where it is surprisingly less crowded—and thank God for that. The steady hum from the various machines filling the space is as good as music to my ears right now, but then again, anything is better than Leslie's annoying ass.

Row after row of treadmills, stair climbers, and ellipticals face an endless wall of mirrors as large TVs above silently play the news, *Family Feud,* and an episode of *Friends.*

I decide to take my chances on a treadmill conveniently positioned in front of the TV playing *Friends* reruns. I pop my headphones into my ears and press play on Bad Bunny's album *Un Verano Sin Ti* for the umpteenth time. I press a few random buttons on the treadmill until the machine finally springs to life.

I gaze up at the TV screen, maintaining a steady walking pace. It isn't long before I am chuckling to myself. I've watched these episodes so many times I don't even need to hear them to know what's going on.

My smile quickly fades at the sight of Leslie's big head walking past me.

And there goes my peace and quiet.

Ignoring her, I keep my eyes fixed ahead as she casually hops onto the treadmill a few spots down from me.

She stretches her arm out toward me, fully aware that I am watching her from the corner of my eye. She flashes her middle finger in my direction before powering her machine on, her body bouncing gracefully as she goes straight into a jog.

I purse my lips and glare at her before raising the speed on my own machine. My weak ankles wobble for a moment as the rest of my body adjusts to the sudden movement because, seriously, when was the last time I ran anywhere?

I can hear the beeps from her treadmill as she raises her speed again, picking up her pace and going into a full run.

She glances back at me with a mischievous smile painted across her lips.

Fuck her and her ridiculous abs. Why couldn't she get fat after having kids?

Against my better judgment, I slide my fingers up the screen, increasing my speed to catch up with her. My lungs have been completely against this from the moment I started pressing buttons, and the sports bra I'm wearing offers little to no support for this amount of activity right now. Suddenly, I notice a man stopped in front of my treadmill.

No, not a man, a god. Motherfucking Thor incarnate. My eyes widen as they stare at the way his white t-shirt clings to his broad chest. My mind can't help but imagine the contours of tight muscle that must lay underneath.

I notice his perfect plump lips, surrounded by a neatly trimmed blond beard, moving as if forming words. The pounding in my ears and reggaeton beat in my earbuds drowns out any other sound.

When I reach his eyes, his gaze burns into mine with an intensity that feels strangely familiar.

Forgetting myself, I come to a complete standstill as I rack my brain, trying to place him. Next thing I know, I'm hurled forward, and my face is connecting with the moving belt of the treadmill. Everything goes black—but not before the last thought in my mind is that of a green-eyed Thor whose gaze had no business burning into my soul the way it did.

4

———

CHASE

"Oh, shit," I gasp, lunging forward and pulling the red safety key out of the treadmill. The machine immediately shuts off as my heart pounds in my chest, and I kneel down beside the crumpled figure sprawled on the floor. She lies there, motionless, her body stretched out and her face turned to the side and partly covered by her hair.

A cooler, more suave guy would probably say he has this effect on the ladies, right? Yeah, not words I'd use to describe me.

Pressing my fingers against the pulse in her neck, I watch the gentle rise and fall of her back before brushing her hair out of her face.

My heart skips an actual beat in my chest.

I knew it was her.

Izzy Peña.

Talk about a blast from the past.

I haven't seen her in years, not since high school graduation, and that feels like a lifetime ago. I watched her a lot that day and the weeks before, knowing they'd be the last, knowing she would leave this place for good and never look back, especially not for me—some kid who was too shy to ever talk to her but happy to take whatever scraps of kindness she'd give.

A woman a few treadmills away rushes over.

"Izzy! Izzy! Oh my God, is she breathing?"

"She's breathing. Just knocked herself out," I respond, trying to play it casual.

"Of course, her dramatic ass would. Fuck. What do we do? Should we move her? Call an ambulance? You know what, let me go get my mom. She'll know what to do."

She dashes off before I can say anything, and Izzy lets out a soft moan.

The sound sends a wave of heat right up my spine. I clear my throat as she begins to stir. I place a reassuring hand on her shoulder as she moves to sit up. I can't imagine waking up on the floor of the gym with some creep ogling you.

"Are you okay?" I ask, leaning down to meet her eyes. She shakes her head and squeezes her eyes shut for a second before blinking a few times. Her eyebrows press together as her long lashes flutter open. When they lock on mine, I can't help but hold my breath, wondering if—just maybe— she remembers me too.

Nah, she won't. It's not like we were friends. I was the charity case she subscribed to for no reason other than pity, I'm sure.

Though, that was never how she made me feel.

Her sweet smell fills the small space between us, unlocking a memory of me in third-period Algebra class, sitting behind her and leaning over my seat, trying to breathe in her intoxicating scent.

She still smells as sweet as summer.

"Izzy, what do you say we get you up off the floor?" I say.

She frowns, confused. "How do you know my name?" she asks, her voice slightly raspy. She leans forward, wincing as she rubs the side of her face.

It feels like a punch to the gut, but I'm not surprised. I wasn't the most memorable kid in school, and thanks to the gym and an extra hundred pounds, I definitely don't still look like the scrawny punk I once was. Deciding not to admit that we went to school together, I clear my throat and answer her question.

"Some girl called your name when you fell. She ran off to get your mom," I say, scratching the scruff on my chin.

"Shit. Quick, help me up. My mom can't see me on the floor like this, or I will never hear the end of it."

She drops her hand from her face and attempts to stand. The angry red blotch on her left cheek makes my stomach sink. Without even thinking about what I'm doing, I reach out and touch the side of her face with the palm of my hand, lightly brushing the inflamed skin with my thumb.

She sucks in a breath at my touch, and I immediately draw back.

What the fuck am I doing?

"Sorry," I mutter.

Those dark, sultry eyes of hers stare up at me, and I look away.

"We need to get some ice on that," I finally say, tearing my eyes away and rising to me feet. I nod toward the front of the gym. "There's a first-aid kit up front. We can kill two birds with one stone—get you ice and away from your mom for a minute."

"Yeah, okay." She attempts to stand up, but a sharp gasp of pain and a quick shutting of her eyes has her sinking back down.

"Let me help you." I drop back down and offer her my hand.

"I'm fine, really. I think I got up too fast," she says, but I don't move my hand away.

She stares at my open palm before letting out a drawn out sigh and sliding her small hand into mine. I pull her up carefully as electricity courses up and down my arm, burning through our point of contact.

Her body sways back as we stand, and I instinctively wrap my free arm around her waist to steady her. She squeezes her eyes shut and brings a hand up to the side of her head. I have to fight myself from lifting her up into my arms and carrying her.

"You sure you're okay?"

"Yeah, just my entire left side feels like it got hit by a car," she admits.

I glance to the front desk. I'd be saving her a whole twenty steps of obvious pain if I just carried her.

Without a second thought, I bend my knees slightly and slip one arm under Izzy's legs and the other behind her back, lifting her up as I straighten.

"What—what are you doing?" she stutters, placing a hand on my chest. "Are you crazy? You can't carry me there!"

"Why not?" I ask, confused.

"Because..." Her eyes widen as if the answer to my question is that obvious. I gaze down at her with a furrowed brow and follow her gaze as it traces the length of her body in my arms.

She rolls her eyes, "Fuck it. Carry me away, Thor," she says dramatically. I shake my head as I chuckle to myself. Her arms wrap around my neck, and her sweet scent engulfs every one of my senses as I force my legs to move forward.

These twenty steps are going to be a lot harder than I thought.

I glance down at her and notice her tight-lipped smile.

"You okay?"

"Mm-hmm"—she nods her head—"but you should probably come with a height requirement." Her arms squeeze around my neck tight.

"You aren't scared of heights, are you?" I tease.

"Not usually, but I've never been carried off like some damsel in distress."

"Technically, you are a damsel in distress. You're in good hands, I promise," I assure her, enjoying the feel of her in my arms a little too much.

"Says every serial killer to his victim," she whispers.

"Whoa. How did I go from Prince Charming to serial killer? But I mean, if I were one, don't you think I would have had my chance when you were lying on the ground, unconscious?"

"I have trust issues, okay? And you could be leading me to my death right now. Away from all these witnesses," she says, glancing around the half-empty gym.

A soft laugh escapes my lips. "You're safe with me, Izzy. Besides, this place has got cameras in every nook and cranny." She eyes me curiously but doesn't say anything else as her fingers curl around the ends of my shoulder-length hair, sending a shiver down my spine.

We reach the front desk, where the receptionist stands flirting with Ant, a personal trainer and total tool. Spotting us, her eyes widen in alarm.

"Chase, is everything alright?" she asks, frowning as she eyes Izzy curiously.

"Yeah, we're good. Just need some ice and the first aid kit. Oh, can you grab a bottled water too, please?"

"Should I get Damon?"

"No, I've got her." I walk past her and head toward the trainers' offices behind the reception desk.

"First aid kit is in the cabinet. Let me know if you need anything else, then," she says, following behind me and placing a bottled water on the desk. She turns toward Izzy, still in my arms, and places a hand on her shoulder. "You poor thing. You are in good hands, okay?" To which Izzy just gives a tight-lipped smile.

"Thanks, Bri," I reply as she heads back to the front desk.

I set Izzy down on the desk and grab the first aid kit from the storage cabinet along the wall. I dump its contents out on the desk beside her, rummaging through all the gauze and Band-aids until I find what I'm looking for—ibuprofen and an instant cold pack.

I tear open the packet of ibuprofen and hand it to Izzy along with the bottle of water.

"Thank you," she mutters as I activate the cold pack, squeezing and shaking it until it finally gets cold. I hand it to her, and our fingers brush against each other, sending that electric shock back up my arm.

Her breath hitches in her throat, and I know, without a doubt, she felt it too.

We both pull away at the same time, and I shove my hands into my front pockets.

She keeps her gaze locked on me, studying me with a curious intensity. I can't help wondering what it is she sees as every nerve in my body tells me to look away before she sees right through me.

"Chase, huh?" she asks, tilting her head to the side and pursing her plump lips in thought. "I don't know, I think Thor suits you better. You've got the whole tall, blond, and broad-chest thing going."

"I don't mind being your Thor," I blurt out, instantly cringing and regretting my words.

Who the fuck even says that?

"I mean, if tall, blond, and broad chest is what you're into." I clear my throat and scratch my jaw, watching her face break into a wide smile. My stomach flips, and I feel like I'm seventeen all over again.

"You were saying something before, weren't you? I remember seeing your lips move, but I couldn't hear you through my headphones."

Izzy? Izzy Peña from Roosevelt High?

My cheeks heat up, and I glance down at her untied shoelace. Instead of admitting I actually knew her from school and feeling that sting of disappointment all over again, I take the bitch way out instead. "Your shoe was untied. I was just trying to warn you."

"Some good that did me." She chuckles softly as I shake my head, replaying the image of her falling all over again.

"You're laughing now, but I was pretty sure I had killed you there for a few seconds."

That, of course, makes her laugh even harder. The sound easily tugs on the corners of my own lips, coaxing a genuine smile to spread across my face.

The frantic calling of Izzy's name outside of the office snaps us out of our bubble. We both look toward the doorway.

"Great, they found me," Izzy whispers unenthusiastically. I take a step back from Izzy as a woman with tan skin, bright red cropped hair, and an outfit coordinated to the one on the lady who had rushed off when Izzy first fell bursts into the room.

"Isadora Leticia, you nearly gave me a heart attack! Are you alright, mama? Let me see you." She places both hands on Izzy's face, who looks less than thrilled right now. The woman inspects her face, grimacing at the red blotch on her left cheek.

"I'm fine, Ma," Izzy says, pulling away from her grip.

"This is not fine, Isadora. You could have a concussion. Do you feel any pressure in your head? Nausea? Dizziness? How many fingers do I have up?"

"Mom, stop. I'm fine. Look." She holds up the ice pack. "Thor has been really helpful and got me ice and ibuprofen. I'm good, Mom. Perfectly fine."

"Thor?" both women say in unison. I feel their eyes sweep over me, and I muster a smile.

"Chase," I correct her, waving my hand in the air. I notice Izzy trying to stand and immediately rush to her side. "I got you," I assure her as she leans into my arm, and I frown at the thought of her really having a concussion and it being my fault.

"I bet you do," snickers the other woman.

"Shut up, Leslie," Izzy barks.

"Don't you two start right now," Izzy's mom says, giving them a warning glare before turning back to me with a warm smile. "I'm Lourdes, but everyone calls me Lulu. Thank you so much for helping my baby girl. She has always been a little bit clumsy, this one," she says, gently pinching Izzy's cheek.

"Mom," Izzy murmurs, glaring at her.

"Leslie, come help your sister."

I take a step back again, giving them some more space as each woman takes Izzy by the arm and guides her out. Izzy turns her head as she passes me and offers me a tight-lipped smile. She mouths the words *thank you* before continuing with her mom and sister out the door.

I open my mouth, but nothing comes out. It suddenly feels like high school graduation all over again. Like this is the last time I'll see her, and I never even told her how, if it wasn't for her and her kindness, I might not have made it through school.

"Oh, and Thor, I'll be sure to leave you guys a review for your exceptional service." Lulu's words hang in the air as they all walk out the doorway without looking back.

"I don't work here," I mutter to myself, confused.

5

IZZY

First time I step foot in a gym in years, and what do I go and give myself?

No, not sore muscles or calories burned, but a damn near concussion.

The entire left side of my face, from my temple down to my jaw, is still radiating in pain from the impact it made against that godforsaken treadmill belt. Oh, and let's not forget Thor's doppelgänger coming to my rescue.

Ah, I can't believe I kept calling him Thor out loud!

Clearly, I've suffered some sort of brain damage, though Mom's quick medical assessment when we got in the car determined I was fine. I mean, she is the nurse here, but still, I think I need a full exam—CT scan, neurological workup.

"You should have seen her straight flirting with this guy," Leslie's voice carries through the small kitchen as she updates our younger sisters, the twins, Layla and Lydia, all about my most recent mishap. She dramatically places the palm of her hand over her forehead, fluttering her eyelashes, and collapses into Layla's arms. "Thor took such good care of me."

Loud cackling laughter erupts off the walls. Even Mom joins in, lowering her voice an octave. "And he was all, like, 'I got you.' Had our Izzy all googly eyed. You see? What did your momma say?"

Leslie, Layla, and Lydia chime in all together, "'The best way to get over a man is to get under a new one.'"

"But I didn't mean it like that!" Mom cackles, bending over in laughter.

I bite down on the inside of my cheek and press the ice pack over the side of my bruised face a little harder. Its soothing coldness provides relief as it cools the heat radiating from my skin right now.

I hate being the center of attention. It's always made me so uncomfortable, and obviously, being the butt of the joke is no fun either, but somehow I always seem to find myself here.

I try to remind myself that they are just teasing me, like they always do about everything. It's just the way they are, and I should not let it affect me. But still, no matter how hard I try to brush it off, it chips away at me.

Deciding I have had enough, I stand abruptly, making the chair screech against the hardwood floor. "Oh no, Izzy, do you need a hand? Thor isn't here to rescue you," Layla teases. I ignore her and storm out of the kitchen, shutting out their voices.

"Oh, don't be like that. You know we're just messing with you," Mom calls out, her voice filled with amusement. I don't hear their comments as I walk into the living room, nor do I hear them all follow behind me until I collapse onto the sofa, and their bodies all topple over on top of me.

"Don't be mad at us, Izzy boo!" Lydia cries out.

"You know we love yo stank ass," Leslie chimes in.

"Why do I have to be stank?" I question as I struggle to breathe underneath their weight.

"Can you two go one second without arguing?" Mom asks. Her and Leslie rise up, relieving the crushing weight, while the twins stay planted on top of me.

"I can't breathe."

"Tell us you love us!" Layla demands.

"I can't stand any of you!" I shout out.

"Say it!" Lydia screams from on top of me, tickling my ribs.

"Fine! I love you! Now get off of me," I cry out, finally giving in.

They get up, both pleased with themselves, and fall onto the couch beside me as Mom answers a knock at the door. She swings it open, her face beaming like a schoolgirl as Luis, her fiancé, walks in and leans down to kiss her.

"Ew!" Me and Layla scream and cover our eyes.

"There are children present!" Lydia says, clearing her throat.

"Well, then the children can go to their bedrooms," Mom says, placing another peck on his lips.

Luis smiles and walks over to greet the rest of us with a kiss on the cheek. "Whoa!" He rears back at the sight of my face. "What happened to you?"

"Oh, you didn't hear? She got into it at the gym," Layla goads.

"I did not!"

"Don't be spreading lies," Mom scolds, popping Layla in the back of her head.

"I fell on the treadmill," I explain.

"Ouch. Are you okay?" Luis, asks, concern etched on his face.

"Lu, you didn't bring her in for a scan?"

"No, I didn't, Doctor Castro. She didn't have any signs of a concussion."

"You should have called me."

"Don't worry about me. I'll survive."

"If you want to stay home tonight, we can go out tomorrow," Luis says to my mom.

"No, no, no, please take her!" I plead.

Mom laughs and wraps her arms around Luis's neck. "Sounds like I'm all yours, *Papi*."

"Ewwwww!" Me and Layla scream together.

"I just have to shower and change real quick," Mom says, ignoring us.

"Just grab a change of clothes. You can shower at my place," he says, wrapping his arms around her waist and gazing at her like she is all he sees.

"I can do that. Why don't you come help me pick out an outfit for dinner."

"If we ever make it."

"Is this what it's going to be like when they live together?" Lydia turns to me and my sisters grimacing at the sight of the love birds in front of us.

"OH MY GOD. Can you guys get a room already?" Layla screams, covering her face with a throw pillow.

"Gladly," Mom says, taking Luis' hand in hers. They giggle up the stairs like a pair of lovesick teenagers.

"And remember, there are children up in this house and paper-thin walls," Lydia cries out.

"Speaking of children," Leslie says, looking up from her phone. "Twins, y'all are on babysitting duty tonight. I have to clock in downstairs in a few minutes."

"Why are we always watching your kids? They have another aunt, you know." Layla stands, pointing at me.

Lydia stands with her. "Also, for the millionth time, we aren't twins and would prefer to be spoken to as the individuals we are."

"Lydia, that's too much work. You loved being called *twins* when you were in training bras a year ago, and Layla, because I said so. Damn!" Leslie stands and makes her way downstairs to the finished basement turned her bedroom.

"Can you two go now so I can finally get some peace and quiet?"

"Peace and quiet? What the hell is that?" Layla says.

"Feel better, Izzy," Lydia says before heading up the stairs.

"Sweet dreams, Izzy. Don't let thoughts of Thor keep you up all night," Layla teases.

"Har, har, har. You're so fucking funny. Now get the fuck out." I get up and reach for the basket under the sofa with my bedsheets and make my bed for the night.

"So annoying," I mutter under my breath.

"You love me."

"Barely," I grumble as I fall onto the couch. The vinyl protecting the sofa crackles beneath me as I move.

I reach for my phone and decide to call Mya.

Thirty minutes later, Mom and Luis have snuck out for their date/sleepover, and I'm cradling my phone in my hand, still talking to Mya, who has thoroughly enjoyed a good laugh.

"I can never go back there!"

"That gym is right around the corner from your house, Iz. What if you bump into him?"

"I have never seen him in the neighborhood before, so I doubt it."

"Girl, if it wasn't for work, you would barely leave the house. For all you know, you could be neighbors," she teases.

"Stop! I would notice someone like him, okay?" Though, I can't shake the feeling I got when I looked in his eyes. The familiarity in them. Like somewhere along the way we've crossed paths before.

I shake my head no, certain that we haven't.

"Well, at least this bump to your head finally has you moving on from he-who-shall-not-be-named. Now, tell me more about Tall, Blond, and Godly."

"Moving on? What? No," I stutter, my heart palpitating in my chest as denial runs rampant through me. "He was just a nice-looking guy at the gym who happened to not be a total tool for a few minutes. He's probably a brainless meathead."

"First of all, a brainless meathead wouldn't have taken the time to make sure you weren't severely hurt. And second, would moving on really be so bad?"

"Okay, fine. He must have a big old heart made of pure fucking gold for falling to his knees and helping my clumsy ass. And to answer your question, yes. Yes, it most definitely would be so bad because I will just end up right here. Heartbroken. Again. I'm not doing this anymore."

"I bet you Thor most definitely does have something big and meaty, though," she says, chuckling.

"Mya!"

Her laughter erupts on the other side of the phone.

"He was just doing his job."

"All I'm saying is you aren't doing yourself any favors by locking up your heart like this. Just because *cara de culo* was too much of a selfish, overgrown man-child to see the amazing, badass woman he had the fortune of sharing four years with, doesn't mean someone else won't see it. A real man will appreciate your selfless heart and love you the way you deserve, Izzy boo."

But why couldn't Esteban have been the one to see it?

That one thought alone drives the knife lodged in my heart forward. Pain, still so fresh, tears through me. I close my eyes and take a steadying breath as my heart continues to bleed out. Pictures of Esteban and his new girl fill my mind. Their smiles and the stupid endearing look in his eyes as he gazed down at her in their last post. I shake my head and try to force them out of my mind and focus my thoughts on anything else but him, her, and all the things we will never ever be.

"It's just not worth the risk, Mya—all the dreams and years wasted on someone and the chance that, in the end, I'll be here again, starting over." *I can't go through this again.*

And for some reason, I'm taken back to a forest of green..

My skin still burns from where Chase's hands had been, wrapped around my hips as he carried me across the gym like I weighed nothing.

"You know what you should do? Go back there and hire Thor to be your personal trainer."

"What?"

"Look, I'm on their website right now. A personal trainer is available to you at no cost. Your mom already paid for your membership, so you might as well put it to use."

"Are you even listening to me?"

"I'm listening, and I am not saying to fall in love...at least not right now. But I am saying a girl has needs, and some rebound dick couldn't hurt."

I laugh out loud at that. "Someone like him would never be into a girl like me, especially not for something like that. He probably has gym bunnies with matching abs for that."

"Excuse me, but 'never be into a girl like you'? What? Gorgeous inside and out, smart, kind, funny as hell, and thicker than a Snicker? Girl, Thor wouldn't know what to do with himself."

"You have to say that."

"I sure don't, but you damn sure need to start believing all of that and more, babe. Also, fuck that bitch-ass ex of yours for making you believe you are anything short of amazing, because you are, Izzy. Now let me hear you say it."

I sigh, mumbling, "I'mabadassbitchwhokicksass."

"I'm sorry? I didn't catch that. Say that shit like you mean it!"

"I'm a badass bitch who kicks ass."

"Again!" she yells into the phone.

"I'm a badass bitch who kicks ass!"

"Damn right you are. So, as soon as you are feeling better, we can work on my post-baby body and head to that gym."

"No, we are not."

"Are to. Love you, bye."

She hangs up before I can say anything else, and I toss my phone down onto the marble coffee table. I stare up at the popcorn ceiling as Mom's bougie crystal light shudders under the weight of the boys jumping from their bunk beds upstairs.

My head throbs painfully as a loud thud shakes the entire house, making me jolt upright.

What in the hell?

Knowing it came from the boys' room, I rush up the stairs, taking them two at a time. I pass Lydia and Layla's room just as their door swings open.

"What was that?" Lydia asks, her eyes wide.

"You were supposed to be making sure they stayed in bed!"

She sucks her teeth. "They were in bed when we checked on them."

I push the door open, hoping to catch those little monsters in the act.

My breath catches in my throat at the sight in front of me. The top bunk bed teeters dangerously on one post as the bottom bunk looks like it has caved in on itself.

"What the—"

"We weren't doing anything," Alfonso and Aiden say in unison as their mother walks into the room, her headset still on her head.

Her eyes widen in shock as she takes in the scene.

"How?" she shrieks, balling her hands into fists. The boys visibly flinch, their shoulders jumping up to their ears as they look at her with wide, innocent eyes.

My eyes land on Liam, the only one who looks apologetic. "I'm sorry," he mutters under his breath, unlike the other two, who jumped straight into denial.

"You two, downstairs, now! And you"—Leslie points at Liam—"Mom can deal with you tomorrow," she says before stomping off.

"I know," he says, dropping his shoulders and turning into his bed.

"At least you still have a bed to sleep in tonight," I say.

He doesn't respond but turns around and faces the wall, covering his head with his dinosaur comforter.

Liam is the youngest of us at just seven years old. He came in way under the radar when Mom had just completed her nursing degree. I still remember all of our shock—hers included—when the stomach bug she was so sure of turned out to be the fifth month of pregnancy with little Liam.

I sit down next to him, brushing his soft curls back.

"You okay, sweet boy?"

He doesn't respond.

"Do you want me to tuck you in?"

"No, you can go now."

"Are you sure?" I ask, letting my fingers dance up his neck.

"Mm-hmm." He sniffles, and my heart cracks.

"Baby boy." I wrap my arms around him and pull him into me as he bursts into a sob.

"It isn't fair! They always get me into trouble, and I wasn't even jumping. I told them not to, but they never listen! How am I supposed to be the man of the house when no one ever listens to me?"

I rub the palm of my hand over his back reassuringly.

"Those are some really big shoes to fill. You have your entire life to be the man of the house."

"But Dad says I'm the man of this house and need to watch out for all you girls." I roll my eyes at his father's words.

"You tell your dad that us girls have been doing just fine without one. And you promised me you would never ever grow up, so what is this old-man talk?" I tickle his ribs until he's giggling and begging me to stop.

"Izzy, please!"

"Promise you'll stay little forever!"

"I promise!" he wails.

"Good." I pepper kisses across his face and tuck him in.

"Is Mom going to be gone all night?" he asks.

"Yeah, bud. You know how excited she gets about date night."

"Okay." I don't miss the quick twitch of his bottom lip. My heart can't help but ache for my little brother, knowing myself what it feels like to be in a house full to the brim with people yet feeling so fucking alone it hurts.

"Move over," I say, pushing his bedding back and sliding into his twin bed.

"What are you doing?"

"Going to sleep, obviously. That couch is killing my back," I say, closing my eyes.

His little arms stretch across my chest, squeezing me as tight as he possibly can.

"I love you, Izzy."

"I love you more, sweet boy."

"I love you most."

"Impossible. I loved you longer."

"Fine," he says, yawning, and not another minute later, he is fast asleep.

I close my eyes as my body gives in to the soft mattress. Even with him already sticking to me with sweat, I might just be able to get a decent night's sleep.

6

___

CHASE

Something is wrong with me.

It's been over a week, and I can't get her out of my head.

Those dark eyes and full lips of hers have been flashing through my mind on repeat from the moment she walked away from me, wondering if she's okay.

I've been perched at every corner of this gym, watching and waiting for her to walk through those tinted glass doors, like some deranged stalker, just hoping to catch at least a glimpse of her long, dark ponytail.

"You competing for the next bodybuilding competition, bro? You've been here every day this week," Damon says, smacking my shoulder as I release the two-hundred-pound weight I'd been pulling on.

"What's going on with you? Is it Nora? She on another bender?" Damon asks, wrapping his tattooed biceps around the frame of the reverse delt fly machine I'd been sitting at.

"When isn't Nora on a fucking bender?" I grunt as if he should know better than to ask that. I mean, he really should. Nora, my mother, hasn't been sober since...shit, probably since she was pregnant with me—I hope.

I reach for my bottled water on the floor beside the machine and take a swig.

"It's nothing," I tell him, hoping he'll let it go.

"Bullshit." Of course, he can't let it go. Like he always has, Damon can smell my bullshit a mile away. We've been best friends since high school, and he is the closest thing to a brother I could ever have.

I let out a sigh, dropping my towel on the floor. I know he won't leave me alone until I tell him. "I was hoping to bump into someone I met last week," I confess, wrapping my hands around the handlebars and dragging the weights back. The strain in my shoulders and upper back screams from the burning pain in my overworked muscles—a reminder of the torture I've been putting them through today. Focusing on my breath, I power through, pushing myself until I go numb.

"'Cause that's not what stalkers do," he mumbles under his breath.

"Fuck you." I breathe out.

"She must be hot if you're forgoing a rest day," he says, looking up, his dark eyes scanning the room as if he'd be able to pinpoint her. "Is it the girl who face-planted on the treadmill?"

"Yeah. I think she left here thinking I worked here, so I just want to clear that up." I decide to not tell Damon we actually went to high school with her. The chances of him remembering her, or any other girl we went to school with, are slim since he spent the majority of all four years pining over the most popular girl in school, who never once acknowledged his existence.

"I mean, you are here as much as the staff, but okay. I see the game we're playing," he says, rubbing the palms of his hands together in excitement. "I like it. You need me to grab you a trainer t-shirt from the back?"

I shake my head. "I'm not playing any games, Dame. So you can wipe that look off your face, okay? I just want to clear the air and maybe set her up with Ant." Though, the thought of Ant touching Izzy as he *"helps"* her stretch sends a surge of jealousy through me that I can't explain. I reach forward, moving the pin to add another twenty pounds to the weight and push the handles back, ignoring the fire spreading across my shoulder blades.

"Man, fuck Ant."

My thoughts exactly.

"What is she looking to do? Trim down? Muscle up?"

"I didn't ask," I grunt, my mind picturing the kind of body she only hinted at underneath the oversized t-shirt she was wearing.

"Well, if you're going to be playing *personal trainer*, you need to know what you're doing. Luckily, you have me in your pocket to help guide you."

"I told you already. I'm not playing a game. I'm not even entertaining this thing with her."

"Oh, so there is a thing." He stands back and crosses his arms in front of himself, waiting for me to continue.

"No. It's just me. I don't know, maybe I just need to get fucking laid."

Yeah, that must be it.

"Don't tell me it's been since Jenna."

I let the weights slam down against each other and don't respond. Instead, I grab my water and towel off of the ground and head toward the locker room, trying to shake that goddamn name from my thoughts. He knows it's been that long. Well over a year since that woman, and time has done little to numb the ache her memory brings. The good times—which, thanks to Nora, were few and far between—and the bad ones, which again were usually brought on by Nora. I should have seen Jenna's ultimatum coming, but still, the fact that she put me in that spot still rubs me the wrong way. Her or Nora, it wasn't even a choice. What kind of son would I be to turn my back on my mother?

"Damn, man. That's not right. No wonder you're here every day, trying to burn off all that pent-up frustration," he says, following me to my locker.

"You're a jackass. You know that, right?" I say, grabbing my gym bag and slamming the locker shut.

"Hee-haw, motherfucker," he jokes. "But for real, tell me about this girl. You know I respect bro code to the end, man. And if you don't tell me, I could end up talking to her without knowing it's your girl."

My girl? I think to myself while walking out of the locker room with Damon hot on my tail as I try to dodge his badgering. My sneakers suddenly skid to a stop, and my hand juts out to Damon's chest, stopping him as well.

It's her.

My eyes take their time trailing over her body as she walks over to the elliptical machines. The faded black t-shirt she wears ends at her waistline, teasing a glimpse of skin, while tight black leggings hug her curves.

I watch her as she laughs, her wide lips stretching across her face. The sultry, velvety sound of her laughter carries through the gym and fills my entire body.

"Earth to Chase," Damon says, waving his hand in my face. "And I'm the jackass," he mumbles before turning around and following my gaze.

He whistles low. "Go talk to her," he says, nudging my shoulder.

"I can't." I turn around, not wanting her to catch me staring at her like the creep I'm apparently becoming.

"What is this, high school all over again, O'Rourke?"

No, it most definitely isn't, I try to remind myself.

"Stop being a little bitch and get your ass over there, or I will."

I turn around and find her eyes already locked onto mine. Those deep-hooded eyes of hers, a pool of infinite darkness.

And now I'm a goddamn poet?

Her lips curve upward hesitantly, and she raises her hand up in an awkward wave as Damon murmurs beside me to go. I move my feet toward her, my mind racing with what the hell to say with each step.

Sorry for being a creep, but can I take you out sometime?

Take her out and then what?

Between my twelve-hour shifts at the animal hospital, chasing my mother's drunk ass around town, and then cleaning up after her, I can't offer much else outside of these walls. This is the one break I get, and what do I do with it?

Abuse my body until it's numb.

The ghosts of relationships past whisper in my mind and the one choice I could never make. Before I know it, I'm in front of her, my six-foot-two frame nearly swallowing her whole. I can feel the woman beside her eyeing me, but all I see is Izzy, and I can't look away. Her eyes trail up as she cranes her neck back and meets my gaze. Her lips pull up in a soft smile, and two dimples appear on either side of her cheeks, tugging at my heart strings.

"Chase, right?" she asks, narrowing her eyes. The fact that she remembers my name sends a wave of excitement through me.

"And here I was pretty sure you forgot all about me," I say, unable to contain my smile as I bite my bottom lip.

"I did hit my head hard," she says, pointing to the faded bruise on the side of her face. I wince at the sight of it marring her skin.

"But I guess, you're harder to forget," she continues, looking away for a second.

I swallow hard, searching my brain for something else to say to that, but I can't think of anything else other than the fact that maybe she's been thinking about me too.

"Excuse me, Thunder God?"

I perk my eyebrows at the woman beside her, just a few inches taller than Izzy with large, probing eyes.

"Mya," she introduces herself as Izzy bumps her arm. "We were hoping you offered some personal training and could maybe help us avoid anything like that happening again, but the receptionist up front didn't know who you were. Gave us an appointment with Anthony for tomorrow."

My throat goes dry as they both eye me suspiciously.

Perfect, I can come clean and resolve this whole misunderstanding.

"Actually—" I start before Damon cuts me off and smacks my shoulder.

"Bethany up there is new. She's still training and doesn't yet know all the things we offer here." I turn my head slowly, glaring at the side of his smug face as he continues to speak.

Don't you do it.

"I'm pretty sure her name tag said Brianna," Izzy says, raising an eyebrow at Damon.

Damon shoots his hand out with his card in between his fingers, like some sort of magician.

"Damon Chambers, personal trainer and manager of this fine establishment lucky enough to be graced by you beautiful ladies tonight," he says, eyeing Izzy's friend seductively.

"Mya. Happily married, new mom, and best friend to Izzy here." She smiles at him and then cuts her eyes back to me. "So..." She pauses.

"I'm sorry, do you prefer Thor, Thunder God, or is there something else you go by?"

Izzy bumps her shoulder and widens her eyes at her.

"Chase is fine," I say, stretching my hand out to shake hers. My large hand engulfs hers, but she doesn't let that intimidate her and squeezes tight. I apply just the slightest pressure in return to hopefully reassure her and maybe get me some brownie points.

Brownie points for what? We are not entertaining this. Just say the truth and go home!

"Then you can train us both together?"

Damon cuts in. "Chase here is one of our most sought-out trainers. Unfortunately, with adding Izzy here to his schedule, he'd be booked up." He turns to me and winks while I stare back in horror at his words. I'm not a personal trainer. And sought out? By whom? The starving cougars who throw themselves at me like it's part of their cardio?

"We want to make this personal and don't just offer help here at the gym but also come up with a personalized workout plan and nutrition education to each individual client we work with. I, however, do have availability in my schedule. We could even find times that work for the both of you to come in together."

Damon has lost his mind. *Personalized training and nutrition education?* I don't know anything about any of this shit.

Mya and Izzy glance back at each other.

"How about a one-month trial before committing to anything long term? Won't cost you anything but your time. What do you say?" Damon asks, offering his best salesman smile.

"That doesn't sound bad at all. What do you say, Izzy? We gettin' our sexy back?" Mya playfully shimmies her shoulders in front of Izzy, who shakes her head, hiding her amusement.

"Remind me why you hate me."

"You'll be thanking me later." She winks at her.

Damon bumps his shoulder into mine, clearly pleased with himself.

"Great, let's get some paperwork signed for liability, and then we'll take you back to record some numbers and get a plan worked up," he says, turning to walk them over to the reception desk. I sit back for a second and take in a deep breath in an attempt to rein in this urge to reach over and punch Damon right now. A few steps away, Izzy glances back, curiosity etching across her face as my heart dances in my chest, pushing me toward her.

7

———

IZZY

Goddamn you, Mya. She shows up at my mother's house unannounced, dressed for the gym, and suckers me here with the excuse of getting her sexy back, even though she definitely doesn't look like she birthed a whole human just a few months ago. And now she leaves me alone with *him*. Even worse, though, are the measurements and scale I'm going to have to face in front of him. I've been heavier than that stupid ideal weight chart my entire life and have come to terms with the fact that I will never be in that range. But damn, it doesn't make the thought of stepping on that scale any easier.

My stomach clenches tight at the thought before the mountain of muscle beside me distracts me.

"Mt. Joy?" he asks, nodding at my chest. "Never been before." He drops the gym bag hanging from his shoulder.

"It's a band."

"Oh, what kind of music do they play?"

"Alternative indie."

"Really?" he says, surprised.

My eyebrows raise. "What?" I've always had an eclectic taste in music but can never help feeling defensive over my music choices. Literally the one time Esteban and my family ever got along was when they were ragging on my so-called *gringa* ears.

"It's nothing," he says, smirking. And as cute as that smirk looks across his lips, I react. My hips jut out, and my hand goes into a balled fist at my side.

"What, because I'm Hispanic, I'm only allowed to listen to reggaeton and salsa?"

"What? No, no. That's not what I meant at all." His eyebrows pull together as he takes a step forward. The sincerity and concern in his eyes immediately make me regret my quick temper.

"You just never pegged me for the alternative type."

"We just met. What would you know about my music tastes?"

"I actually have a confession to make. We went to school together, like from elementary all the way through high school."

"What?" I say, quite utterly confused.

"Yeah, you, uh..." He pauses and scratches the back of his neck before continuing. "I don't even think you'll remember, but you shared your lunch with me a few times. You even helped sign me up for the free lunch program in middle school."

"Keagan?" My eyes widen as the memory pops in my head. "Shut up!" I playfully push against the wall of muscle on his chest. "Why did you say your name was Chase?"

His eyes shine bright as he grins sheepishly. "Chase is my middle name. I started going by it after high school."

"Wow!" The Keagan in my memories was a scrawny, string bean of a kid who was always falling asleep in class and sitting alone at lunch, no lunch box or friends in sight.

"I can't believe it's you. Like, you really just kept on growing after high school, huh?"

He smiles, and a storm of raging butterflies swarms my stomach.

Nope. This is a butterfly-free zone.

I glance at the scale and decide I'd rather deal with that enemy than this traitorous feeling right now.

"How about those numbers?" I place a foot on the scale when Chase stops me.

"Hold on," he says, wrapping his large hand around my wrist, completely engulfing it. My skin ignites from the contact.

"Why don't we forget the numbers for today and do something easy?" He nods at the doorway. I step down and follow him out.

"Also," he says, leaning down as we walk back into the gym, "I really didn't mean to offend you before. Indie, country, rap...you listen to whatever you want. I still play Eminem's "8 Mile" track like it's 2002," he says proudly.

"Of course you listen to Eminem," I say, rolling my eyes.

He smiles down at me, and I can't look away. Like a kid staring up at the sun, knowing all too well it will hurt, I can't look away from him, and my heart revels in the burn sure to come.

Jesus. What am I saying right now? No. Look away, Izzy. Look away!

"How about we steer clear of the treadmills and just walk the track?"

"I can walk."

We fall into an easy silence as we walk through the gym.

"Were you just leaving?" I ask, remembering the gym bag he was carrying.

"I was on my way out, but I don't mind staying for you."

"For me?" I cock an eyebrow.

No, not for you. He's just being nice and doing his job.

"I—" he stutters, and his cheeks grow pink.

Holy hell, is Thor blushing? My own face flashes with heat as he pushes the words out. "I was kind of hoping I'd bump into you again," he confesses, making my stomach flutter. My mouth goes dry, and I choke, going into a straight coughing fit.

"Are you okay?"

"Yeah," I wheeze, still coughing into my hand.

"I'll grab you a water," he says and runs off.

I squeeze my eyes shut and try to breathe through the tickle in my throat.

Seriously, that mother-effing—

"Here." He's back faster than I expected with a bottled water already opened for me.

Tears fill the corners of my eyes as I reach for it and shamelessly guzzle it down. The refreshing sensation washes over my dry throat.

Chase's hand falls onto my back. "You okay?" he asks, concerned.

"Yeah, just something in my throat, I guess. Thank you for rescuing me again, Thor." I raise the nearly empty water bottle in the air.

"Anytime, Isadora."

"Not Dora. *Dorra.* Roll those r's, Thor." I chuckle, enjoying teasing him and his sad attempt at saying my name correctly a little too much before scanning my eyes over every piece of metal machinery. All of it makes my stomach twist and turn as I imagine the pain I'll be in. Hell, even biking and my ass swallowing that tiny seat will be a bitch I'll feel for the rest of the week.

"Is that why you go by Izzy?"

"It's just easier, I think. Still way better than my middle name—which, had my mom had her way, would have been my first name."

"Let me guess, does it start with an L?"

I laugh out loud at that. "How'd you guess?"

"Lulu, Leslie..."

I cut in, adding my siblings' names, "Layla, Lydia, and Liam."

"Elevator or stairs?" he asks.

I give him a knowing look that I'm hoping portrays, *Boy, if you haven't figured me out yet...*

He smiles and, without another word, presses the button for the elevator.

"I swear I'm not completely allergic to physical exertion. I've spent plenty of days subbing for gym teachers." The double doors open, and we step in.

I've never in my life battled claustrophobia. I mean, growing up in my house, sharing every space with another person is the only life I knew, but suddenly these four walls and Chase take up all the air surrounding me. It's too much. His scent all around me invades my senses, making my body tingle. It takes everything in me to not close my eyes and moan.

"So, what's your L name?" he asks, distracting me from my thirsty-ass mind.

"Leticia."

He rolls his lips into his mouth and nods as he fails at suppressing his laughter.

The elevator doors open right onto an actual running track. From downstairs, it didn't look that bad, but up here now, I realize just how big it really is. It spans the entire circumference of the building with three wide rows taped to the black-and-red flooring that curves around a metal railing, supported by sturdy metal beams and transparent glass panels. I step out of the elevator and onto a rubberized surface that provides both cushion and support.

"Whoa." This was definitely not what I was expecting.

"So, who do you have to thank for naming you Isa-dorra instead?" And the butterflies are back.

"My dad. It was a family name, I think, but he passed away when I was little, and his side of the family never stayed in touch after."

"I'm sorry."

"So, how'd you get into personal training?" I ask, desperate to change the topic.

"Um, Damon sort of pushed me into it, I guess."

"And you're a teacher?" he asks.

"Second grade."

"That's amazing."

"Eh, I'm not saving the world."

"But you are," he says, stopping abruptly. "For some of those kids, you're their second home. I can't imagine the level of patience and compassion you must have. Don't sell yourself short on the impact you're leaving."

Well, damn.

"Thank you," I say.

"Oh, your shoe's untied," I notice.

"Shit, thanks." He bends down to tie it. "So is yours," he adds.

"Saving me again, Thor." I chuckle as I bend down. As I pop back up, so does he, and our foreheads knock into each other. Both of us groan in pain.

"Are you okay?" Chase asks, placing his hand over mine that is currently rubbing my head.

"Shit, you've got a hard head."

"I could say the same to you," he says. "Are you okay, though?"

"I don't know how much more injury my head can take."

"This poor, pretty head of yours..." he says, rubbing the pad of his thumb over last week's yellowing bruise.

Pretty head? He thinks I have a pretty head?

I gaze up at him, suddenly realizing how close our bodies are. His tall frame keeps his face an ocean away from me as his piercing gaze makes it feel like it would take nothing at all to close the distance between us.

Aww, shit. This is bad.

Chase clears his throat and takes a step back, shoving his hands into his pockets.

"Ready?" he says.

Ready? No, I don't think I am. I mean, I can't be, but what if I tried?

"Izzy?"

"Yeah, I'm ready," I say and push my legs to move forward.

"That's two miles," he says, raising his hand in a high five.

And for some reason, I give him a fist bump instead, cringing at my fucking awkwardness. *Seriously, why am I like this?*

"How do you feel?"

"Fine. I can handle walking."

"Okay, next time we'll kick it up a notch and jog." He glances at his watch. "I have to be somewhere in a few, but we should probably exchange numbers and come up with a schedule, right?"

"Yeah, that makes sense." I reach for my phone in the pocket of my leggings and unlock it before handing it to him to input his info.

"Okay." He taps his number into my phone as we walk back over to the elevator and hands it back as the doors open. We get in alongside a pair of women whose shorts and sports bras leave so damn little to the imagination they are basically underwear. They shamelessly eye Chase and whisper to each other as they giggle and stick their asses out more than they already are.

Gag!

I shake my head and tuck myself into the far back corner of the elevator. I chance a glance at Chase, who leans casually against the elevator wall with his hands tucked into his pockets. I expect to find his eyes on the asses in front of him but am surprised to find them locked on mine.

His heavy gaze takes the breath from my lungs as my pulse thuds in my ears.

The elevator doors open, and we all shuffle out.

"This was nice," Chase says, stopping in front of me.

"Yeah, it was really great catching up."

"Same time tomorrow work for you?" he asks, and I nod my head.

"I'll confirm with you tomorrow in case you change your mind," he says, walking backward and smiling wide like I just made his day.

I watch him walk across the sidewalk until he disappears around the building.

"You need me to get you a napkin for all that drool? You're damn near panting over Thor like a bitch in heat," Mya's voice comes from beside me as she bumps into my shoulder.

"Oh. My. God. Really, Mya. You are worse than my mother!"

"What you mean to say is thank you. And you are welcome, boo," she says, hooking her arms with mine as we walk out of the gym. It's late, but luckily, the parking lot is lit up by bright LED light poles. I squeeze Mya's arm tight as a crisp breeze wisps by and we reach our cars parked next to each other.

"How did your session go?" I ask.

"I'm already sore as shit from one workout, but I feel really good. Like I'm kind of proud of myself for even trying to keep up with Damon. He's a machine. What about you?"

"It was fine, just walked and talked. Do you remember Keagan from Roosevelt? Really tall and skinny?"

"Always falling asleep in class, right?"

"Yeah, well, Keagan is Chase."

"What! Damn, talk about a glow up."

I chuckle to myself as I think about him again. He was always very quiet and never once shared anything personal with me. It's not like we were friends or anything, but still, I hope whatever his situation was then got better.

8

CHASE

"Get out of my house, you no good—" I don't flinch as the plate in her hand crashes against the wall near my head.

"Nora," I say her name, exhausted with this bullshit and the mess I'll have to clean up.

Another plate lands at my feet, and I curse myself for not putting those dishes away earlier.

Mental note: Add goddamn paper plates to the list.

"You stay the hell away from me, Keagan! I don't want you here!" she says through gritted teeth. "I hate you! Do you hear me? I hate you! We don't need you here. Go!"

She doesn't mean it.

I know she doesn't.

This isn't her. It's just the fucking alcohol—and who knows whatever else—that is raging through her system right now.

But damn it if her words don't make it feel like the hard-

66

wood floor might just give out underneath me and swallow me whole.

I rub my face with the palms of my hands and take a deep breath in and out. "Mom," I beg, even though I know it's pointless. She doesn't see me—her only son and the last person in her fucked-up world that hasn't given up on her.

No, all she sees when she looks at me is the face of a ghost, a man who did exactly what she is begging me to do right now. But unlike him, I can't do that.

I may be the spitting image of my father, but I am not him.

"It's me, Mom," I plead as she picks up the last plate on the dish rack.

I quickly reach up and release my hair from its hair tie, letting my hair fall to my shoulders, and lift my hands in the air in front of me. "It's Chase, Mom," I say, taking slow, deliberate steps toward her.

Her blue eyes glare daggers into me.

How can she not see me?

"Mom, please. Put the plate down," I say as softly as possible.

Her eyes flutter as the venom I just saw in them dissipates, and she comes back to me.

"Chasey boy? Where have you been?" I reach for the plate in her hand and place it back in its spot.

"I've been right here, Mom," I choke out. She reaches up and places her cold hands on my cheeks as she looks up at me. My eyes fall closed as I try to hold on and savor this fleeting moment with her.

She tsks, and my heart sinks, knowing exactly what will come next.

"It's such a shame how much you look like him."

I nod my head in agreement, taking the blame as I do always. I mean, maybe if I didn't remind her so much of him, she wouldn't have spent most of my life using alcohol to forget him.

"Let's get you into bed, Mom. It's late."

"I just need something to drink." She turns and heads straight for the cabinets. They swing open with a loud creak. One by one, top and bottom, her hands dart from each handle as she quickly scans each shelf.

"Where is it?" she calls out behind her, slamming the last cabinet shut. The sharp sound bounces off the walls around us.

"What did you do with it?"

"Do with what?" I ask as I pick up the shards of plate off the floor and toss them into the trash can. I know what she's looking for, but I won't tell her I threw it out with yesterday's trash.

"You know what, Sugar Bear, I'm going to run to the store real quick, and I'll pick up some paper plates. Then we won't have any more messes to clean up."

"It's the middle of the night, Nora. Everything is closed."

"Well, that's no fun." She stands there with her hands on her sides, watching me continue to pick up the mess she made.

Then, like a light going off in her head, she smiles excitedly and runs off into the living room. I drop the last piece into the trash can and watch her find a bottle of whiskey under a loose floorboard on the stairs.

Shaking my head, I open my notes app and add wood floor glue to my growing list.

What Nora needs is rehab, not a bottle of whiskey to nurse her to sleep.

It's not like I haven't tried that already, but the hard truth is she doesn't want the help, nor does she want to quit drinking.

With her bottle in hand, she walks to her bedroom, swaying slightly as she takes a swig from the bottle.

I watch her and can't help the feeling of contempt and resentment that washes over me. She doesn't look back or even say goodnight as she slams her door shut, locking herself and her precious bottle of liquor in with her.

Taking the stairs two at a time to my bedroom, I let out a sigh of relief as I fall into my bed. My sore limbs and tired eyes weigh me down as I sink into the soft bedding.

Instead of letting sleep take me, I open my phone and read over the information Damon sent me when an incoming text comes in.

Unknown Number: You really saved your name in my phone as Thor?

I can't even contain the smile on my face as I add her into my contacts.

Me: I mean, you're the one who insists on calling me that.

Isadorrra: Well, I don't know anyone else who has had a full-on Avengers glow up after high school so…

Isadorrra: Also, I did not think you would be up. I just wanted to confirm that.

Isadorrra: for later.

Isadorrra: Sorry, good night.

Isadorrra: And good morning.

Me: Thanks for the confirmation.

Me: Can't sleep?

Isadorrra: Something like that.

Suddenly I want to know anything and everything that might be keeping her up at night.

Me: Care to share?

The dots at the bottom of the screen come and go before her next message.

Isadorrra: I fell asleep in my little brother's bed and woke up in a bucket of his sweat. So, another shower later, here I am, scrolling social media per usual. What about you?

Me: Reading.

Isadorrra: Anything good?

Me: Nope. Just some personal training stuff.

Isadorrra: Oh. You must really enjoy what you do.

Me: Eh, I sort of fell into it.

Isadorrra: Before we move forward, there is something I have to tell you.

Isadorrra: I hate the gym and all things dieting and have always failed miserably at both. I mean, obviously I've never succeeded, and if it wasn't for my mom's wedding, I would definitely not be stepping foot in a gym now. So, yeah, I just feel like I should be transparent with you about that.

Me: Okay. Well, instead of worrying about what you couldn't do in the past, how about, moving forward, we focus on what you want to do from here? It doesn't all have to suck. If you hate burpees, then no burpees.

Me: Also, we should give the treadmill a rest for a bit, respectfully.

Me: I hate diets too. Getting healthy should be about changing your lifestyle for a better one that will sustain and nourish you. Balancing all that with indulgences every now and then is key to maintaining goals.

Me: Also, #TacoTuesday counts as a solid and very allowed cheat day in my book.

Isadorrra: You make this all sound so easy, but #Taco-Tuesday is LIFE. I guess I can get down with this if you're telling me I don't have to eat like a rabbit for the next month.

Me: Stick with me, and you might even come to enjoy it.

Isadorrra: HA! Never!

Me: Never say never, Dorrra.

Isadorrra: So, then I'll say never, ever, everrr, Thor. I should get to bed. I've got an early start and a gym sesh I need to prepare for.

Me: Same time okay with you?

Isadorrra: Yup. We should probably go to sleep, like, right now if we are going to be functioning by the end of the day.

Me: Good point. Goodnight, Izzy.

Isadorrra: Goodnight, Chase.

The next day, I walk into the gym surprised to see Izzy already there. She stands up front, talking with Damon.

"There he is. The man of the hour," he says, grinning from smug ear to smug ear like he knows something I don't.

"Sorry. I got held up at work."

"You have two jobs?" Izzy asks as she eyes my navy scrubs and gym bag.

"Um." Shit. I thought I would have had enough time to change before she got here.

"Yes. I have another job that I work when I'm not here." I internally smack the shit out of myself for not forming words stronger than the crap I just spewed out. "I'm just going to change."

"I'll warm her up for you, *Thor*," Damon says, winking at me as I try to bite down the image of him *warming* her up.

I yank the locker door open and change out of my clothes as quickly as possible. Walking out as I pull my t-shirt on over my head, my bare chest smacks right into someone's face.

My arms shoot out and grab the person before they fall back.

Izzy.

"Is there any part of you that isn't hard?" she mumbles under her breath. I release my hold on her and fight the smirk working its way across my lips as her eyes bounce over the muscles of my chest. My skin heats up as her gaze lowers, tracing the contours of my abs as I pull my fitted shirt down.

"Are you okay?"

"Huh?" she mutters, her gaze fixed on my chest.

I'd be lying if I said I wasn't enjoying how flustered she looks right now.

"Sorry, um... Damon was going to get my weight and measurements before he got distracted," she says, pointing behind her.

"I can get your measurements," I say and turn toward his office.

I nod to the scale beside the door as Izzy groans.

"Do we have to?" she says, looking like a toddler ready to throw a tantrum.

"We don't have to do anything you don't want to do. Remember, it doesn't all have to suck, but these numbers will help in seeing progress and tweaking the training so you can see the results you'll be working toward."

"Fine," she says, kicking off her sneakers.

"You can keep your shoes on."

"Nope, not giving this deceiving, square trap of lies any more ammo than it needs," she says, holding her breath and squeezing her eyes shut.

"What are you doing?"

"Did you get it?" she asks, keeping one eye closed to look up at me.

"Get what?" I ask, confused.

"The lies from the square trap. Keep up, Thor."

"Yeah," I say as I quickly scribble the number down. "I got it." I turn the clipboard over before laying it on the desk.

"Good. Don't tell me. I don't want to know."

"Okay." I don't want to make her feel any more uncomfortable than she already is.

"Now what?" Her brows furrow as she crosses her arms in front of her chest.

"Hey. That number doesn't define you."

"I know that," she says, looking everywhere but at me. "Can we please just get this over with?"

"Yeah. Can you spread your arms out?"

She huffs, biting her bottom lip as she stretches her arms out for me.

I take the measuring tape and try to remember exactly where Damon had said to place it before wrapping it around the midpoint of her arm. I jot down the measurements quickly before repeating it again on her other arm.

Her eyes bounce around the entire space, and I notice her holding her breath every time the tape touches her.

When I wrap it around her waist, she sucks in a breath, practically jumping out of her skin, and I can't take another second of this torment.

I drop the tape and stand up, placing it on Damon's desk.

"I think we're good here."

"You didn't even finish."

I dip my head down, trying to catch her gaze. "It's not important if it's going to make you feel like you want to crawl out of your skin."

"I'm sorry," she says, now looking down at her shoes.

My hands reach out and pull on the bottom of her chin, tipping it up until her eyes lock with mine.

"You have nothing to apologize for, Izzy. Fuck that little square trap of lies."

"Thank you," she says, her eyes shining up at me as if I said exactly what she needed to hear. I allow myself an internal pat on the back as I move my hand down.

I walk her out of the office and to an empty space near the weights on the gym mat where we start the workout Damon planned for me. Now all I have to do is keep my eyes off of her and my hands to myself as much as possible for the next thirty to forty-five minutes.

I can survive not being a total creep for that long, I reassure myself as she leans forward, accentuating her curves, and pushes her chest out as she stretches one foot behind her.

My body, of course, betrays me as my dick twitches at the swell of her breasts.

Fuck, this is going to be harder than I thought.

9

—————

IZZY

*F*uck. This. Shit.

I can't. I just can't do it.

Chase was being nice the first few days. He even offered a rest day on Sunday, but somewhere between Monday and today, he kicked it up all the notches, and my body is spent.

Every single one of my muscles is sore. It hurts to laugh, to breathe, and I have failed miserably at trying to pee standing up because my thighs quiver and threaten to give out any time I attempt to squat down.

It's not even like the workouts were crazy hard. Mostly cardio with a weight here and there, but we were burpee free...until today—right now to be exact.

"I can't—" I pant as my arms buckle, and I collapse onto the mat on my stomach. My face sticks to the gym mat as sweat trickles down my forehead. The t-shirt I'm wearing feels like a hot blanket weighing me down and clings to me like a second layer of skin.

I can't do this!

"Yes, you can. Get out of your head, Izzy."

I shake my head and squeeze my eyes shut.

Why am I even putting myself through this?

"Because you can do hard things, Izzy. Come on, we're almost there," Chase says, and I pop my eyes open as I feel him lean over me. I take in a deep breath of air but get his delicious woodsy evergreen scent instead, which honestly is way better. Those warm green eyes of his lock onto mine before dipping down to my lips, like I swear they have been doing every single time he looks at me.

I can't be imagining it.

"Just one last set," he says low, his voice wafting over me like a cool breeze. It gains the attention of every damn cell in my body. My nipples tighten and push through the thick padding of my sports bra.

"Come on, Iz. You didn't get this far to just give up now."

I groan in protest as I will my body to move. Holding myself up by my arms and the tips of my sneakers, I drop down in a half-assed attempt of a push up, then bring both my feet forward and jump up in the air, barely managing to swing my arms past my ribs.

"That's it. You've got it. Keep going," Chase says, counting down from three as I force myself back down on the mat as fast as possible so I can get this the hell over with.

"Three."

"Keep going, you're almost there!"

"Two."

"One."

"Yes! You did it!" Chase shouts. When I jump up from the ground into my final fucking jumping jack, he immediately wraps an arm around my waist, and thank God for that because I'm pretty sure I would have crumbled in a heap on the floor if he hadn't.

"I've got you," he says, peering down at me as I pant like a wild dog. I grip his arms and get lost in his touch.

"Breathe," he says, inhaling slowly, but I can't think, let alone breathe, with him so close. Not with his touch burning through the thin layers of fabric between us.

What is wrong with me today?

"Izzy?" he says, concerned, and I attempt to shake the lust from my thoughts.

"I didn't push you too hard, did I?"

Push? Oh God, do I know somewhere he can push hard.

Down, girl!

"No, I'm okay," I force the words out. Placing my hands over his chest, I immediately regret the movement because I don't want to take my hands off. But I need air, and I definitely need to put some distance between Chase and my horny mind right now.

Reluctantly, I pull away and stumble over to the nearby bench.

"Whoever invented burpees can burn a slow death in hell for this shit, though," I pant as I sit down and chug from my water bottle.

Chase chuckles as he walks over and joins me on the bench.

"Royal Huddleston Burpee."

"What?" My face crunches in confusion as I swipe the water that dribbles down my chin with the palm of my hand.

"The guy who invented the burpee," Chase says, raising an eyebrow as if this is common knowledge.

"Why?" I ask before bursting into a fit of laughter. Chase's own laughter erupts with me.

"I might have said the same thing as you a while back—before I started taking my fitness more seriously."

"You're telling me you didn't come out of the womb doing burpees?" I tease.

"Ha, ha. You know I didn't. I was a literal string bean most of my life, and burpees still suck, even now. I can't lie about that, but it is a very efficient workout, and you killed it, Izzy," he says, wrapping his Hulk-like arms around me and squeezing me to him. God, it takes everything in me to not moan out loud as I let my tired body sink into his warmth.

"I'm proud of you," he says, rubbing the palm of his hand up and down my arm, making my stomach twist into knots.

"Don't you two look cute," my mother says, walking in with a Cheshire smile across her painted pink lips because yes, even at the gym, her makeup, though more subdued than usual, is still on point.

I quickly shrug out of Chase's embrace as he stands and walks over to his water.

Mom's greedy eyes waste no time tracing over his sculpted figure.

"What do you want, Ma?"

"Are you almost done? We still have to get ready for tonight."

I roll my eyes, letting my head fall back against the brick wall behind me.

"*No comience.* You're coming. The couch needs a night off, and you need to stop acting like a spinster."

"Mom!" I whisper-shout, widening my eyes at her in hopes that she stops being so embarrassing. I glance toward Chase, who still has his back toward us, and rush to my mother's side.

"Okay. I'll meet you in the car."

"Why don't you invite your friend?" she says loudly, peering over my head.

"Shhh. We're not friends. He's just my trainer."

"I can show him something he can train. Hard," she says, clamping her teeth together.

"You are literally getting married in a month. Really?"

She laughs. "I'm kidding. Besides, he clearly only has eyes for you." She winks, bumping into my shoulder. I turn around, catching Chase's eyes on mine before he busies himself with his phone.

"Can you go? Please," I beg her.

"Ten minutes," she says, turning around. I don't miss the extra swing in her hips as she passes Chase, sending a wave of jealousy sinking deep in the pit of my stomach.

"Wild plans tonight?" Chase asks, walking toward me. I walk to the middle of the mat and turn to face the mirrors.

Spreading my legs wide, I lower my upper body as I stretch the way he showed me.

"Bachelorette party for my mom. Yes, as you can imagine, it will be wild as fuck. Please pray for me," I say, catching his heavy gaze on my lower body in the mirror. I push my ass out a little further as I switch legs.

God, am I my mother's daughter, or am I my mother's daughter?

I shake my head at myself and drop down into a calf stretch. When I look back up to the mirrors, Chase's eyes are on mine, heating my skin.

"Don't bring your knee in front of your hip like that." His voice comes out thick. "Lie down on your side, arm out." I comply instantly while my insides melt at this commanding tone he takes when he's in training mode. He kneels down behind me, his hands grasping my hip and leg, maneuvering them into the proper stretch I was failing at, and I'm a goner. The lust-filled thoughts in my mind scream at the sight of him in the mirror behind me and what he would look like naked just like this, pushing into me and stretching my body past all its limits.

I'm lost to the image in front of me and the R-rated ones distorting my mind. His lips move, but the only sound I hear is the steady drum of my heart wreaking havoc against my ribcage.

I'm supposed to be coming down from my workout, not feeling like I'm running a 5k.

"Lie back," he demands, and damn if those two words don't make my thighs clench together.

His eyes lock on mine as he places my legs over his shoulder. Gripping my thighs in his large hands, he leans down over me, and I suck in a breath as my muscles twist and pull against the pressure of his weight above me, stretching my tight joints past their limits.

"Is this okay?" he whispers.

I nod my head, biting my bottom lip, too afraid I might just moan—not from the pain, but from the liquid desire coursing through my veins right now.

He doesn't look away as he holds the stretch, and that delicious burn spreads from my hamstrings up to my core, and the moan I have been trying to suppress finally escapes. My hands rush to cover my mouth.

Chase stills above me, his eyes locking onto mine—golden orbs darkening right before me. My heart thuds loudly in my ears as I stare at him, completely mortified.

"Am I hurting you?"

I shake my head, embarrassed.

He drags his eyes to my hands, narrowing them as if they've offended him, then drops my leg, straddling me as he places his hands over mine, pulling my hands away and up above my head. His tongue sweeps across his bottom lip, and he stares at my mouth as if he's dying for a taste.

"And is *this* okay?" he whispers. His mint breath skates across my skin. My breast heaves against his chest, and I nod my head again because there is no way my muddled mind can form words.

"You have to say it, Izzy," he says again, pressing himself against me.

"Oh, God, yes." I push my hips forward, feeling his hard length.

Lost to the burning forest in his eyes as he leans down, I send a silent prayer to Jesus that this man takes me right here, right now on this gym mat.

But of course, a crash interrupts us, and we both tear our gazes away to the commotion as a lanky teenage boy struggles to lift a large weight off the ground. His cheeks turn red when he glances up, and the realization of what the fuck we just did hits me.

What the hell was that?

Chase and I both scramble up off the gym floor, and he rushes over to help the kid with the heavy weight, lifting it with ease. I glance around the open gym floor and notice eyes burning into me, clearly enjoying the show they were just about to get.

A wave of embarrassment crashes over me and sends me dashing to grab my phone and water canteen before I rush out of there.

I need air.

I need water.

I need Chase to finish whatever we were about to start back there.

No.

No, I am not fucking my trainer.

I am not fucking anyone.

10

CHASE

I knew this was going to be hard.

Not the training part, which, thanks to Damon's help, has gone off without a hitch. Also, taking Izzy's cues to make changes to the workout plan that wouldn't discourage her. I've actually really enjoyed coming up with ways to help her reach her goals and watching her get stronger and more confident in her workouts.

It's the keeping-my-goddamn-hands-to-myself part of this that has proved to be the hardest thing I've ever done, and I am failing miserably at it. What started as completely innocent soft touches here and there to help guide her into proper forms when we first started have somehow turned into me almost taking her right on the gym floor.

I should have my balls kicked in for the way I came on to her. Even through my thin gym shorts and those fucking baggy sweatpants she is always wearing, I know she felt it.

Fuck.

I can't get the sound of that moan out of my head.

And the *yes* that fell from her plump lips, giving me the green light to keep going.

Green light for what?

To fuck her right there on the dirty gym floor while everyone else watched?

I am not an exhibitionist, but I am pissed that I didn't at least get my lips on her before we were interrupted and she ran off.

I crossed the line.

She thinks I'm her goddamn personal trainer, for Christ's sake!

Fuck.

I open our messages, the last one being hours earlier, when I admitted to her how I had actually never watched an Avengers or Thor movie.

I was, however, into the comics as a kid and still own a few classics.

I type and delete and type and delete again, unsure of what the fuck I even want to say.

Hey, sorry about pressing my dick against you, but you did give the green light. Would it be cool if I kissed you and maybe took you out on a date?

What the fuck am I? Thirteen?

Shit.

It's late. I've been home for a couple of hours and still have to go find where Nora is holed up for the night. Izzy is out anyway, probably dancing the night away and forgetting all about it—the almost-moment I'm sure she regretted the second she came to her senses.

Suddenly, the small blip with three dots appears in the corner of our text, then disappears. I sit up from my spot on the couch and stare at the screen, willing her to come back and type out whatever she had to say.

The blip returns again, and I hold my breath, waiting until it disappears again, and a picture comes through. A picture of her at the bar with her mom as she sticks her tongue out and holds a drink up in her hand.

She looks so completely different from how I've seen her at the gym. It makes my mouth fall open.

Her long hair falls in soft waves over her shoulders, past her breasts, which are barely contained by the low cut of her top.

Fucking gorgeous.

I stare at the screen for another second before finally tapping out a response.

Me: You're stunning.

Isadorrra: Imdrunk.

I smile and glance at the time. It's barely midnight.

Me: Lightweight.

It's another five minutes before she replies.

Isadorrra: You should come and show me a thing or two, Papi Thor.

I read her last message twice more. Fuuuucck me. I want to hear her say that out loud.

My phone rings in my hand before I can type out a response, and I groan at the name on the screen.

"Yeah," I respond, knowing exactly what the fuck it's about. Annoyance surges through me and kills whatever joy I had just felt.

"Third night this week, O'Rourke."

"I'll be there in ten."

"Make it five. She found out we were watering down her drinks and spit in my face when I tried to pry her from the counter."

Shaking my head, I angrily push myself out of bed and shove my feet into my sneakers. Snatching my car keys from the counter, I slam the door so fucking hard I'm surprised it doesn't break off its hinges.

By the time I crawl back into my apartment, I'm so exhausted with another night of Nora's bullshit that I fall asleep on the couch.

She had me out on a wild cat-and-mouse chase all night long, running and dodging me.

By the time I wake up, sometime after eleven, I couldn't be more thankful for a Saturday. Nora won't be up for another few hours, and I can sit and fucking relax.

I reach for my phone and remember Izzy's invitation last night that I never responded to.

God, she must think I'm such an asshole.

I send her an *Are you alive?* gif of Dory from *Finding Nemo* tapping on the screen.

She responds with an *I'm dying* gif of Cameron from *Ferris Bueller's Day Off* in bed.

Me: Need a hangover cure?

Isadorrra: Like the kind of cure that involves more alcohol? No, I think I'll suffer and learn my lesson the hard way.

Me: It's not that much more alcohol and it's not to be enjoyed, but it will cure your hangover so you can at least be somewhat of a human and a little less walking zombie.

I send her the recipe my mother taught me to prepare as a kid and I could make with my eyes closed:

3 ounces of gin

¼ ounce of lemon juice,

2 to 3 dashes of Tabasco sauce

Chile pepper slice

Isadorrra: Yeah, that looks like I'll have to run to the store, so hard pass. Just let me learn my lesson the hard way and suffer.

I get up and walk over to my fridge, knowing I have everything she would need here.

Me: What's your address?

Isadorrra: Are you sending flowers for my grave?

Me: No, I'm bringing you Hair of the Dog. I'm making one already and have enough for another.

Isadorrra: Oh. Had yourself a wild night too, Thor?

Me: Something like that.

She texts me her address, and I smile to myself, realizing she's just a couple of blocks away. I make her and Nora their drinks and leave Nora's on her nightstand before quietly closing the door behind me.

After a six-minute drive, I park my truck and search the row of brick homes for her house number.

"You lost?" a guy smoking a cigarette asks me, sitting on the steps of the house that matches Izzy's address.

I open my mouth to tell him no when Leslie, Izzy's sister, storms out, throwing something at the back of his head. A sandal bounces down the steps and lands at my feet.

"What the fuck, Leslie?" he asks as he rubs the back of his head.

"Who the fuck is Cindy, and why is she hanging around my sons?"

"Cindy? Baby, I don't know who that is. I don't even like that name!"

"Oh really? You want to play stupid with me. Fucking dumbass!"

I turn my head as they argue, feeling like I'm in the middle of something that should be done in private.

"Hey, Thor. What are you doing here?"

I turn around sheepishly.

"Thor? Why the fuck you calling him Thor?"

"I'm here to see Izzy."

"Why?" she asks, raising an eyebrow and ignoring him. Izzy's mom pushes through the screen door.

"What do you mean why? *Chismosa,* let him in. And keep your fighting off my front porch," she says, holding the door open for me.

"Thank you." I nod my head toward her and walk up the steps.

She eyes me up and down before opening the screen door wider for me to squeeze through into a narrow living room. "I thought Izzy said no gym today?"

"Yeah, but I heard it got pretty crazy last night and just wanted to bring something to help with her hangover."

"Aw, that's very sweet of you." She smiles. "It's a shame you couldn't join us last night, *Papi Thor.*"

I swallow hard and clear my throat as heat burns my cheeks red.

She reaches out and takes the tumbler from my hand, opens the lid, and brings it to her nose. "Oof, hair of the dog," she says, making a face. "Good luck trying to get her to drink that." A little boy runs down the stairs and straight into her hip.

"Lulu, I'm hungry," he says, tugging on her shirt. She sucks her teeth and picks him up into her arms.

"Here," she says, handing back the tumbler. "Izzy is upstairs, second door on the left." She walks back out the front door.

"Come take care of the children you two *sinverguenzos* made," I hear her shout behind me. I take the stairs slowly, following the framed pictures along the wall. I notice all the differences and similarities she shares between them and the happiness captured in each shot. It makes my stomach squeeze tight, wondering what it would have been like to be loved like this. To have memories like these. To have people there by your side through thick and thin.

I reach the second door on the left, like her mom had said, and knock twice, hoping I'm not waking her. Worst case, I'll just leave her the drink and head back home, but I really would like to see her and talk about yesterday.

The door opens, and I don't notice the kid who opened it until he speaks.

"Who are you?"

I peer down at him as he cranes his neck to look up at me.

"Hey there, little man." I glance up into the room behind him. "I'm looking for Izzy."

"Why?"

"I brought her some medicine for her headache."

"Are you her boyfriend?" He frowns.

My eyes widen as the words *I wish* flash in my mind.

A female's off-key voice sings at the top of her lungs through the thin walls, belting out words to a song I don't recognize.

"Izzy is obsessed with *Encanto*," the little man says, rolling his eyes. I smile, staring at the door the singing is coming from. I can't say she sings like an angel, but it is cute.

"Is that a movie?" I ask.

"You haven't watched *Encanto*?!" he shouts, his eyes bulging out of his face in shock.

"Liam," Izzy's mom calls out, "your father is here."

The kid groans. "I'll be right back. My dad never hangs out for long, but we can watch all together later," he says.

"Um..." I start. He waits, looking up at me as his mom calls his name again. He gives me a big-dimpled smile that is identical to Izzy's before running down the hall.

What the hell do I do now?

I open the door and walk into the bedroom littered with toys and a bunk bed in the corner. A twin bed in the opposite corner has a woman's shirt and shorts on it.

I place the tumbler on the nightstand beside it and open the drawer for a pen and paper to leave a note on. I'll just leave before she even notices, and hopefully the kid isn't too upset I had to leave.

"Chase?"

I swing my head back toward the door, and my mouth falls open at the sight in front of me, where wet, creamy, bare skin comes into view. My eyes take their time tracing a path up her smooth legs, up her thighs, and over the thick cotton towel. Her wet hair drapes behind her bare shoulders, and her red-rimmed eyes widen in surprise.

"You've been crying." I frown. My feet move before I can stop myself.

"What's wrong?" I ask, reaching forward and pressing the pad of my thumb against a tear at the corner of her eye.

"It's nothing," she says, turning away from me and wiping her eyes with the back of her hand. "What are you doing here?"

I walk back to the nightstand and pick up the tumbler. "Hangover cure, remember?"

"Right. Sorry, my brain has been all over the place today, and this headache is not helping me."

"Did you take anything for that yet?"

She shakes her head. "Not yet. I'm so stupid for drinking so much."

I reach into my front pocket for the ibuprofen I brought over just in case she didn't have any. "Here, take this."

Her gaze lingers on me, and for some reason, it unsettles the shit out of me. I swallow hard, wondering what she sees. All everyone else sees is the muscle, but if I could, in her eyes, I'd show her I'm so much more than that.

"You didn't have to go through all this trouble for me, Chase." She breathes, biting her bottom lip while I surprise myself by reining in the sudden urge to reach out and pull it down.

"You're worth the trouble, Izzy." I extend my arm out toward her. Our fingers brush against each other, and I gently curl mine into the palm of her hand, guiding the ibuprofen into her grasp. "I'll just leave you with that so you can start feeling better," I say softly and hand the tumbler to her next.

"Have you ever had an empanada before?" she asks as she takes the cup.

"A what?"

She smiles. "I'm just going to get dressed, and then I am going to blow your mind, Thor."

She's been blowing my mind from the moment I saw her again.

But my life with Nora has no space for a girlfriend—I learned that the hard way once before. It's fucked, but damn it, I want her. All of her. But how do I get that without hurting her—especially when this is all I can give her?

11

IZZY

*S*hutting my bedroom door behind me, I let my head fall back against it and take a deep, shuddering breath. The tears I'd been able to keep in check in front of Chase now prick the corners of my eyes. It took everything in me to not jump into his arms and seek the comfort I so desperately need right now.

I can't get over how sweet and kind he is to come all this way just to cure my hangover. I was with my ex for four years, and I don't think he ever even bought me a candy bar when I was on my period.

Speaking of my ex, the heaviness that has been weighing on my chest since last night returns all at once, along with the memory of Esteban's latest post on his social media account.

Stupid fucking tears. Stupid fucking heart. And stupid fucking Esteban and his new stupid fucking *fiancée*.

He's engaged...after only seven months...with some random girl. He's engaged.

I hate how much it pisses me off, but damn it, we were together for four years, and marriage had been nothing more than an afterthought. A, *'Yeah, sure. One day, Izzy.'* A 'one day' that would never come, and he fucking knew it. Wasting my time while I doted on him like the future fucking wife I thought I would be. Dragging my naive, stupid heart along for so long.

I take the ibuprofen slowly melting into the palm of my hand and swallow down Chase's tonic. Bringing the metal tumbler to my lips, I take a cautious sip. It has a very dull kick to it but surprisingly it's not as bad as I thought it would be.

I place the tumbler down on the nightstand beside Liam's bed. Tears stain my cheeks as I unwrap the towel from around my chest and bring it to my face. I release a muffled —and very needed—scream into the damp cotton.

My head throbs painfully behind my eyes.

I force my mind to think of anything else, and of course, Chase is the first thing it conjures. He's too good to be true. Esteban felt like that too, and now look at me.

Chase isn't him, I try to remind myself, then I remember I left him alone...in the hallway...where my family can sink their claws into him.

I drop the towel and get dressed in the clothes I had left on Liam's bed. I fan my face a few times before taking the tumbler with me and opening the door. But instead of Chase's smoldering eyes, I'm met with an empty hallway.

Oh no.

"Chase?" I call out. The floor creaks beneath me as I walk

down the hallway. Mom's obnoxious laughter carries over the old-school reggaeton music she refuses to live without.

I ignore the sinking feeling in my chest at the thought of him just leaving without a goodbye and rush down the stairs into the kitchen, skidding to a stop in the doorway.

Chase in Mom's *Queen of the Kitchen* apron makes no sense at all, but damn if he doesn't look good in it. The way his large biceps flex as he rolls the rolling pin over the fresh dough in front of him makes my mouth water. Long legs spread wide apart as he leans over the counter which, compared to him, resembles one made for dwarves. Chase seems to be focused on the task in front of him as my mother shakes her hips to the beat of the music beside him, methodically rolling small balls of dough for empanada disks.

I watch for a second longer, leaning my aching head against the doorway. Chase and empanadas are a pleasant and needed distraction from the dark thoughts swirling around in my head.

"Creeper much?" Lydia, the older of the twins, whispers in my ear as she brushes by me to get into the kitchen. I stick my tongue out at her, and she pretends to grab Chase's ass when Mom grabs her wrist and twirls her into her arms. Dragging Chase into it next, they back him up into the corner of the counter. His flour-dusted hands raise in the air as my mother grinds against him, and my little sister swings her hips in front of her.

His eyes connect with mine. I cover my mouth with my hand, suppressing a chuckle as he mouths the word, *"Help."*

The slight fear and amusement in Chase's eyes is adorable.

Esteban would never be caught in this situation. The few times we did happen to come over *together*, he damn sure never stepped foot in the kitchen. He maintained his distance from my family, claiming they were *too much*. I never pressed it, especially since he and my mom butted heads any time they shared the same space.

My brain throbs painfully, as if just the thought of him is what is causing this suffering and not the rum or tequila running through my bloodstream. I am full of so much regret right now I can't even take it.

I squeeze my eyes shut and rub my temple in hopes it will alleviate some of this pressure.

"Izzy?" Chase calls out, and I somewhat register him squeezing past my mom and rushing to my side. "Are you okay?" he asks, hooking his arm around my waist, steadying me. The warmth from his body mixed with the cool mint from his breath as it skates across my forehead sends a chill up and down my spine.

"Izzy?" he repeats. His voice is etched with concern as he leans down and searches my eyes.

"I told you to watch your liquor," Mom says, pulling a chair out from the dining table and dragging it behind me before checking on the seasoned beef simmering in the pan on the stove.

"Lightweight," Lydia mutters next, earning herself a smack on her arm with the large wooden spoon in Mom's hand.

"And what would you know about being a lightweight, huh?"

"I was kidding! Damn. Ouch, Ma! You could have burned me."

"But I didn't. Now watch your language, little girl."

Lydia rubs her arm and sucks her teeth.

"Why don't you sit down," Chase suggests, but I shake my head. I don't want to move from this spot in his arms. At least here the only thing I can focus on is his hard body.

"I'm okay. I just need a minute."

"Didn't Chase bring you something to make you feel better?" Mom doesn't turn around as she stirs the meat for the empanada filling.

"I bet he did." Lydia chuckles under her breath.

"I have it right here." I lift the cup up, noticing the Norriton Vet logo on it. I take another sip.

"I'm surprised you drank that. You are always the worst with medicine."

"Clearly, it was made with looove, Ma," Lydia chimes in.

"Dee Dee, I swear to God." Usually, it's Leslie pushing my buttons like this. What the hell!

"It was nothing, really. I've been making them forever now," he says, tucking his hands into his front jeans pockets. The movement tugs his pants down slightly, revealing a sliver of smooth skin that catches all our eyes.

"You spend a lot of mornings having to recover from hangovers?" my mom asks.

"Oh, I don't drink," Chase says, walking back to the counter, flattening balls into perfect shaped disks.

"Like, at all?" Lydia asks, unbelieving. I kick her under the table to shut her up and not interrogate the man on his drinking habits.

"Nope. I make these for my mom all the time, though," Chase says.

"Awwww, *que lindo!*" Mom shrieks. "Your mother is lucky to have a son like you. How is it that not one of my five children can do that for me?"

Lydia walks over to the stove, "I mean, if you're lucky, Liam might at least leave the tap on in the bathroom for you," she quips, spooning a bit of ground beef into her mouth.

Chase smiles, but it doesn't meet his eyes the way it did before. Staring down at the counter, lost in thought, the corners of his lips turn down into a frown.

I have the sudden urge to crawl into his arms and kiss that frown off his lips.

Whoa, girl.

"*Papi* Thor, break is over. The empanadas won't fill themselves. Come on."

"Ew, Ma, please don't call my trainer Papi."

"Like you don't want to call him Papi," Lydia mutters under her breath. I glare at her as Chase moves his hands over the dough and I shamelessly watch the delicious muscles in his upper back.

"Buenas, buenas, mi gente." Mya walks in through the living room, a wide teasing smile on her face and Baby Z perched on her hip.

"Z bear! Gimme, gimme, gimme." Mom tears the baby from her arms and breaks down into Spanish baby talk.

"Can you believe there was a time in my life where people actually acknowledged me when I walked into a room?" Mya shakes her head and goes around cheek-kissing everyone before stopping in front of Chase.

"Fancy catching you here, Thor. Is the gym now offering in home training?" she asks, her eyes playfully bouncing between the two of us.

"He was just bringing me something for this hangover," I say, raising the tumbler in my hand.

"Psh, from the hundred and three video messages you left me that I got to laugh through this morning, I am surprised you are even awake right now, girl." She wraps her arms around my shoulders and squeezes me tight.

"Cara de culo isn't worth any of your tears, Izzy boo." She whispers in my ear.

"By the way, I forgive you for missing my bachelorette party. A woman only gets married a third time, you know," Ma jokes as she stirs the ground meat around with Baby Z on her hip.

"Real funny, Lulu, but I am sorry I couldn't make it last night. Kev is out of town for work, and Zion has been up every night with a fever, thanks to all these teeth coming in at once."

"Yo, that's fucked up about Esteban and his girl, right?" Layla says as she enters the room. Her eyes widen when she sees me, and she freezes instantly, grimacing. "Ooh, my bad, Izzy. I thought you were still in bed."

My teeth grind together as I clamp my mouth shut.

In one quick motion, Mom kicks her sandal off her foot, lifts it with her toes, and tosses it up for her hand to catch, all while still holding Baby Z in her arms. "Are you out of your mind?"

"I said *my bad.*" Layla's shoulders lift up as she buries her head in her phone.

"That's your one for today, little girl. Let me catch that mouth slipping again."

"Yes, ma'am."

The room grows silent, besides the sizzling from the pan.

I stand and decide to busy myself with finishing the empanadas instead of sitting here feeling sorry for myself. Chase, who hasn't said a word, is busying himself with filling the disks with meat. I peek over his shoulder and smile at the effort he is putting into it as he presses down on the corners with the pad of his thumb.

"Here, use a fork. It will keep it from opening up when we fry them," I say, passing him a fork. I slide beside him, our arms brushing against each other, and show him how I do it. I hand it back to him and watch him as he tries it.

"Like this?" he asks, his eyebrows squeezing together as he concentrates.

"Perfect."

He beams, proud of himself. His smile is contagious and spreads to my own lips as butterflies swarm my stomach. I don't want to look away, but I know I should.

He's not Esteban, my brain reminds me.

I force myself to turn back to the stove and fry the first set of empanadas. Distracting myself with food instead of my emotions is way easier. My mouth instantly begins to water as the aroma of sizzling dough engulfs the air, filling the room with an irresistible allure.

Everyone else continues chatting behind me, and I tune them out. Methodically, I place the empanadas on the cooling rack and then drop the next batch into the hot frying pan.

"That smells amazing." Chase hums his approval beside me. It sends a wave of goosebumps up my neck.

"I told you I was going to blow you away."

He leans in over my ear, and I turn my head, fascinated with the curves of his lips as he speaks. "You've already been doing that, Izzy."

My mouth falls open as Mom shoves her way in between us.

"*Oye*, move over before you burn my empanadas."

She takes the not-as-golden-brown empanadas out and sets them on the cooling rack. I step back and snatch two empanadas in each hand from the already cooled stack and wrap them in a napkin. The tips of my fingers burn as I hold them all in my hands. I nod my head to Chase to follow me out and lead him out of the house and to the front porch.

"Am I taking this to go?" Chase asks as I hand him his empanada. I sit down on the steps and pat the spot next to me before taking a bite, attempting to both enjoy and cool the steaming piece in my mouth.

Chase chuckles softly as he takes his time to cool his down before bringing it to his mouth. His eyes close as he chews slowly and moans his satisfaction out loud, the sound hitting the spot right in between my legs.

"Fuck, that's good." He groans.

"I know," I say, smiling.

We sit in comfortable silence and take a few more bites before he speaks again.

"Are you going to tell me about Esteban and if I need to go find him and punch his face in?"

The image of Chase pummeling Esteban's smug face in does make me feel better, but the thought that he would go to bat for me like that ignites something else deep inside me.

I release a heavy sigh, mentally bracing myself as my thoughts drift back to the bits and pieces of last night I do remember—when I opened Facebook, only to be immediately confronted with a prompt asking me if I wanted to congratulate the happy couple on their new engagement, followed by a picture of them together, radiating pure fucking joy with *her* proudly displaying a breathtaking engagement ring.

"My ex got engaged last night. It's stupid that I even let it affect me. I think it just caught me off guard, you know." I hate how much the sting of those first few words feels like I rubbed salt into an already bleeding wound.

"Do you still love him?" he asks, his voice soft yet almost forced.

I pause, letting the weight of his question sink in for a minute as memories of the years spent with my ex replay in my mind. Years spent feeling like I wasn't enough while hopelessly waiting to check the next box in life, clinging to the idea that it would somehow fill this void inside of me.

No, that can't be right. That can't be what love looks like... feels like.

"No," I say, shaking my head, without a doubt. The resounding sound from those two letters echoes inside of me, shifting some of the jagged pieces of my heart back to their places.

Chase nods his head as I continue.

"I think I loved the idea of loving him. I mean, this time last year, I thought it would be my wedding I'd be getting ready for. We were together for so long it...it just felt like the next gradual thing to come, even if I wasn't truly happy. But I don't know. I guess in the end I just wasn't enough."

"Don't," he says, grimacing as he shakes his head.

"Don't what?"

"Izzy." He leans in close, his green eyes peering into my soul and holding me still. "You are more than enough." The pad of his thumb reaches out, tipping my chin up and holding my gaze—as if I'd look anywhere else but at him. I couldn't even if I tried.

"It was him. *He* wasn't enough for *you*." The look in his eyes as he speaks makes my heart melt, but his words...they hit me right at my core. I have to blink back the tears in my eyes as his words reverberate through me.

Chase's gaze lowers to my lips. His eyes grow heavier as his lips fall slightly open, and for a second, I think he's going to kiss me.

Oh my God. Yes!

"Well, look at you two." Leslie struts up the stairs, stopping beside me. "You know I am pretty sure the gym prohibits this sort of client-trainer relationship."

"How about you mind your business, Leslie," I say, rolling my eyes as Chase stands, putting so much distance between us. "Me minding my business wouldn't have gotten you Betty back. You're welcome." She drops my car keys into my hand and walks up the rest of the stairs.

"I should head out."

I fight the frown that wants to spread across my face and shove a piece of empanada in my mouth instead, nodding my head.

"I'll see you tomorrow, I-sah-dorra," he says, perfectly rolling his r's over the ones in my name. My heart melts at the sound, and the corners of my lips ache from the wide smile that's working its way up my face.

"You've been rolling your *r's*, Thor."

"Just for you," he says.

Just for me?

12

CHASE

I haven't had a shit day like this in a really long time. Hell, probably since Izzy stumbled her way into my life. She has definitely been a sweet distraction from the everyday bullshit that my life is. I mean, let's face it. Besides her, most of it sucks, and no matter what I do, I can't seem to get anywhere.

"Chase, I need an IV on Princess," Dr. Bianchi calls back before locking himself up in his office. Princess is the ninety-pound beast of a Doberman currently dehydrated in room three. As always, on a Sunday night, I'm the only tech in the office, and the only one Bianchi ever calls to open up shop for emergencies. I don't usually mind, but I doubt Princess, as cute as she is with her sad puppy-dog eyes, is going to make this easy for me. And I'm supposed to be meeting Izzy in thirty minutes.

I haven't seen her since yesterday morning, and I'm nervous. We never even got to talk about what happened last time we worked out together, and since seeing her wrapped in a towel, my mind has been stuck in the gutter, imagining her without it—which is going to make today's workout that much harder. What started off as an old-school crush has turned into something all-consuming, and it's only been a few weeks.

The need to tell her how bad I want her sits on the edge of my lips. Maybe it's time I come clean about everything...or maybe I should just cancel tonight's session.

Damon closes the gym earlier on Sundays, so canceling would make the most sense, right?

Instead, I tap out a quick text to Damon.

Me: I need a favor.

Damon: What do you want?

Me: I won't make it to the gym until after hours. Let me get the keys, and I promise I'll lock up.

Damon: NO FUCKING ON EQUIPMENT OR MATS!

Damon: You know I got you, bro. ;)

I finish entering Nova's chart into the computer and make my way down the hallway to where Princess is resting, stopping to text Izzy with the change in plans.

Me: Did you leave for the gym already?

She sends me a pic of her feet propped up on a marble coffee table, followed by a text.

Isadorrra: Nope.

Me: Had an emergency at work, so I'm running late. Meet me there in an hour instead?

Isadorrra: Fine.

Isadorrra: Also, Ma wants to know if you've ever had *mofongo?*

Me: Mo-what?

Isadorrra: Figured.

Two hours later, I'm jogging up to the gym doors. No thanks to Princess or Bianchi, of course, it took longer than expected. Princess came in barely able to hold her head up, but one look at that needle in my hand gave her a burst of energy, ending with my hand clamped in her mouth. Not the first or last time I end up bandaged up at the end of a night. But of course, I go and make a bigger mistake by stopping home for a quick shower and change when I catch Nora stumbling out of the house.

"Not tonight, Nora. You're keeping your ass inside."

"What are you gonna do? Lock me up, Keagan?"

I shake my head, really not wanting to deal with this right now and toss her over my shoulder.

"Put me down, you shithead!" She pounds on my back.

I toss her into her room and lock the deadbolt I installed on the outside.

"I fucking hate you!" she screams, throwing God knows what at the door.

"Fuck you, too, Mom," I shout back before heading up the stairs. She can tear the whole house up if she wants to.

Damon swings the front door open and tosses me his keys.

"I don't understand why the hell you still work there, man. It was supposed to be a summer gig, not a lifetime commitment. You got enough of that with Nora," he says, shaking his head. We both started working at Norriton Vet in high school. He only lasted that summer after learning the hard way how severely allergic he was to dogs and cats and anything else covered in fur. As for me, I never found a way to leave, and as twisted as it may seem, this job is the only thing stable I have ever had in my life. It made sense to me, at least. Steady income and no need for college or training school when Bianchi was more than willing to teach me everything I needed to know, even if it was mostly so he didn't have to pay me more money than I'm actually worth.

"I owe you."

"Hell yeah you do. I left your girl on the treadmill. And remember what I said."

My girl. My ears like the sound of that a little too much.

"Hey," he shouts back with his windows down. "Remember what I said—not on the equipment."

"That's not going to happen."

He drives off, and I walk into the gym, locking the doors behind me. The cold air from the AC hums through the vents, and the steady drum of feet slapping against a treadmill soothe something inside of me. I walk toward the sound of the treadmill and have to bite my lip in an attempt to suppress my wide grin. I can't explain how I feel when I'm around her. Giddy, nervous, excited, and stupid all at once. I'm dying to make a move, ask her out for real, or just give in to this desire swimming in both our eyes. I saw it yesterday, written all over her face when she looked at me, but for whatever reason—most likely her dickwad ex—she shakes it away.

My hungry eyes trail down her backside, and I take in the tight pair of shorts hugging her hips. They stop at her mid-thigh, exposing the pair of delicious bare legs I have been dreaming of since I caught sight of them in her hallway.

I clear my throat and force my legs and eyes forward.

"I never thought I'd see this day again," I say behind her. My voice comes out way deeper than intended, and Izzy, of course, jumps in alarm. Her hands reach out and grip the corners of the treadmill as I dash forward and immediately tug on the safety string. My other arm wraps around her waist.

"This thing is a death trap!" she wails. I chuckle and reluctantly release her.

"I really don't think it's the treadmill."

"You're right! It's you! At least you had the decency to catch me this time."

"I'll always catch you, Izzy—or at least try. You should know that by now." I smile sheepishly at her, feeling like the clown I am.

Her beautiful brown eyes stare up at me through thick lashes, and her lips fall open. God, it would take nothing at all for me to just lean down and kiss her right now.

Make your fucking move, idiot!

"Izzy." I reach for her hand instead, carefully tracing her delicate fingers and giving her time to move away before interlacing my hand with hers.

Her eyes look down at our intertwined hands before glancing up.

"What happened to your hand?" She covers my hand in both of hers, bringing it up for closer inspection.

"That looks bad."

"It's nothing."

"Doesn't look like nothing to me, Thor." Her moon-shaped eyes search mine as her fingers trace around the wound, which has at least stopped bleeding.

I lick my lips and take a steadying breath.

God, I want her more than I've ever wanted anything. I'm being crazy. Why would anyone want to subject themselves to my bullshit anyway? No one has before.

"Just a Princess bite. I'll survive." I release her hand and take a step back, shoving my other hand into my hair.

What am I doing?

Pretending to be a personal trainer? Setting up after-hour gym sessions? For what? Spending all this time with her? For what?

What kind of life could I even offer her?

"Hey, you okay?" she asks.

"Yeah, it's just been a long day."

"Want to talk about it?"

I stare into her eyes, thinking for a second, *just maybe*. But instead, I'm shaking my head and hopping on the treadmill beside her.

"I'm good," I lie, swallowing the lump in my throat as I start the machine up. My feet instantly fall into an easy jog. I can feel Izzy's eyes burning into the side of my face, but I keep my gaze glued in front of me and speed the treadmill up.

Before I realize it, my feet are pounding against the moving belt, the rhythm of my steps mirroring the thundering of my heart. I don't know how long I'm running before sweat beads gather on my forehead, and my hair is falling into my face.

Izzy's hand is on my arm, her touch grounding me and bringing me back to the present. I yank the emergency strap, bringing the treadmill to a sudden halt. My chest rises and falls rapidly as my lungs crave precious oxygen. Gasping for breath, I straighten my posture, placing my trembling hands on my hips. I squeeze my eyes shut and take slow, deliberate breaths until arms wrap around my waist. My breath hitches in my throat as Izzy catches me off guard. She pulls me into an embrace as her touch electrifies every single one of my senses.

My hands hover hesitantly in the air until, slowly, they find their way to the small of her back, and finally, all the noise in my head fades. All that matters is this feeling right now, right here. I hold onto her, breathing her in like the air I need.

"Izzy," I breathe against her ear, my voice laced with need. She tilts her head back, her face brushing against my chin. Her eyes search mine before trailing down to my lips with a hunger I know for a fact mirrors my own. She leans in, her lips grazing mine, and for the first time in a long time, I let go and let myself fall into this feeling. My lips meet hers, and I take my time savoring this moment that it feels like

I've been craving for forever. It's a memory in the making, one that I will relive over and over once this is over.

My phone sounds in my pocket, but neither one of us moves away as it rings in the empty space around us.

She pulls her lips away from mine for a second too long. "You should probably answer that." I shake my head, wrapping my hand behind her neck and pulling her back in.

"I'll just silence it." I reach into my pocket and pull out my phone, hitting the side button to mute the ringing, when I notice the number on the screen and freeze. I stare at the screen in my hand while a slow, silent dread fills me in that moment of recognition.

"Chase?" Izzy covers my hand on her neck with hers, bringing me back.

"Do you need to answer that?" she asks, her voice filled with concern.

"I think so." I frown, bringing the phone up to my ear. She kisses my chin and wraps her arms around me again, and I release the breath trapped in my lungs.

"Hello?"

"Is this Keagan O'Rourke?"

"Keagan Chase O'Rourke, yes," I respond, correcting the woman on the phone and clenching my jaw at the sound of my full name.

A cold chill snakes its way up my spine as I listen to the dispatcher explain to me the stolen car Nora crashed into a police cruiser and the hospital information of where she was taken—unresponsive.

My mind locks onto the one word the dispatcher used.

Unresponsive.

Nora is lying on a stretcher, unresponsive.

The heaviness I thought I had just shaken away returns with a soul-crushing weight that sucks all the hope and joy I have left.

I hang up and hold the phone in my hand so tight I'm surprised it doesn't shatter in my grip. Izzy, as if sensing the gravity of the situation, holds me even closer, her face pressing into my chest and anchoring me here with her. My body sinks into her warmth as I wrap my arms around her, wishing I could stay right here, for-goddamn-ever. But just like my mind has been trying to remind me since we started this with her, I don't have room in my life for this.

Whatever this is will just end up with her resenting me, hating me, and hurting because of me.

"Is it your mom?"

"She's at Einstein."

"That's just fifteen minutes away," she says, pushing me back. She hops off the treadmill and grabs her water bottle and keys from the floor beside us. "Come on, I'll drive."

"What? No. You don't have to. She's probably fine and just sobering up," I say, scraping my hand over my face.

"Chase, you're shaking."

Shit, am I? With my stomach rolling over, I raise a hand in front of myself, watching it wobble uncontrollably in the air.

How did I not notice I was shaking?

"There is no way you can drive like this. I've got you. Whatever it is. If it's nothing or something, you don't have to be alone."

Too many emotions all at once clog my throat. Words she couldn't know could mean the world to the lonely kid who still lives inside of me.

I nod my head, too caught up in Izzy and her beautiful heart, and follow her out of the gym.

13

IZZY

With one hand on the steering wheel, I maneuver Betty in and out of traffic as we head to the hospital. My other hand remains glued to Chase's, offering a silent source of comfort. I glance over at him, lost in thought as he stares down at our entwined hands with a sad, tormented look on his face. I've never wanted to be there for someone as much as I want to for Chase right now. Though he has shared fragments of his life outside of the gym and his dysfunctional relationship with his mother, I wish he would let me in completely. It's obvious that he's been the only one carrying the weight of her burdens alone for far too long. I can't imagine what that must have been like for him growing up. It makes me wish I would have done more for him when we were in school together. I could have befriended him and offered him my comfort then. Who knows where that would have led us... maybe right here together.

"I'm so sorry, Chase," I utter softly, not knowing what else to say.

"Don't be," he responds, his voice tinged with a mix of anguish and frustration. "If I'm lucky, she's dead. Fuck. I don't mean that." He forcefully shoves his free hand through his hair, tugging at the ends.

My heart aches in my chest as I desperately search for the right words, anything at all that could provide Chase with some level of comfort. I'm used to him being the source of encouragement, not the other way around.

"I just want her to not drink herself into a damn stupor and then get behind the goddamn wheel. That's it. I'm not asking for mother of the year, just a sober one."

"Maybe this will be the wake-up call she needs." I glance over at him with all the hope and light I can offer him.

He shakes his head, rolling his lips back bitterly before staring ahead through the windshield. "Any hope I had in Nora ever getting the help she needed died a long time ago."

A moment later, I'm parking Betty in the first spot I find and switch off the engine. I turn to face Chase, who hasn't made a move to get out of the car.

"Thank you for the ride, Izzy." He covers both of his hands on mine and brings it to his lips, placing a soft kiss on the back of my hand. "I'm sorry our night went to shit before it even started," he mutters.

"I'm coming in with you."

"You don't have to do that," he insists, concern etched on his face.

"But I want to, so let me, okay? Sometimes Thor needs a sidekick too." I give his hand one final squeeze as he stares back at me. A flicker of emotion crosses his eyes.

"Thank you," he whispers, feeling a rush of warmth as his lips brush against the back of my hand again before he releases it and opens the car door.

As he steps out, I desperately try to get myself together before melting into a puddle on the floor of my car.

It feels like so much has changed between yesterday and now. Just twenty minutes ago, his lips were on mine, and damn it if it wasn't the single best first kiss ever.

My heart continues to race in my chest as the alarm bells in my head threaten to ruin everything. Caution, fear, and anticipation of where this could lead.

I try to keep my face relaxed as I meet Chase on the other side of my car. His hand almost instinctively finds mine, intertwining our fingers, and suddenly, the doubts and worries fade into the background. All I can focus on is just how right this feels with him.

Hand in hand, we walk through the sliding glass doors of the emergency room. The sterile scent of antiseptic lingers in the air, and the bustling energy I had expected to see is nothing more than a desolate room.

We walk toward the reception desk where Chase speaks to the woman there who tells him someone will be out to bring him back soon, so we sit and wait.

I don't know how much time passes as Chase gets lost in thought, his gaze fixed on the linoleum while his thumb mindlessly traces circles on the back of my hand.

I can't help staring up at him while my heart and mind engage in a silent battle.

My mind, guarded and cautious, wants so bad to remind me of the heartbreak we are barely recovering from. It urges me to proceed with caution, reminding me of the risks and vulnerability that comes with opening up to someone again. But my heart, the relentless optimist—clearly an inherited trait from my mother—whispers possibility. It encourages me to take this chance on Chase and on all things I foolishly still hope for.

"O'Rourke?" a nurse calls out, her voice echoing through the space. Chase and I stand quickly and make our way toward her. Her curious eyes sweep over Chase before settling on me and then to our joined hands.

"I can only take one of you back right now," she explains. "Once we have her settled in a bed upstairs, visitors will be allowed."

"Oh, okay." I nod my head. Chase turns to face me, a frown pulling on the corners of his lips.

"You don't have to stay and wait. I can get a ride back—"

Before he can form another word, I silence him with a finger pressed against his lips.

"I'm not going anywhere. I'm here with you."

He inhales deeply, nodding in understanding and appreciation. The nurse presses a side button that opens the double doors, and as they part, Chase takes slow steps backward, one hand still clasped in mine. We stretch our arms out between us until only the tips of our fingers touch, lingering in a bittersweet connection. Then, with a final glance, he turns around, the doors closing behind him.

Already missing the feel of his hand in mine, I shuffle back to my seat. Rubbing my hands over my thighs as my leg bounces up and down, a restless energy settles itself over me, and those persistent thoughts take the moment of weakness to come back with full force. I reach for my phone, deciding to distract myself with the digital world. My fingers glide across the screen as I lose myself in the act of scrolling when a DM pops up in my notifications.

Este_Mar_Art: Can we talk?

Now he wants to talk? Seven months later and after getting engaged to some random girl he barely knows, and now he wants to talk.

No.

Fuck that.

I immediately delete and block him, then shove my phone into my wristlet, deciding to stare at the empty walls instead.

The rumble of an engine stirs me awake. I sit up in my seat, confused as the memory of Chase carrying me out of the emergency room comes to me. My eyes widen at the numbers flashing on the dashboard in front of me. It's already midnight? The last time I glanced at the time, I was in the waiting room, and it was a quarter to nine.

I move my eyes over to Chase, who seems to be lost in thought and frowning at the road in front of him. My body is still buzzing from our kiss earlier. I try to tame it down and focus on the broken man beside me. Those strong shoulders of his are slumped forward, and his arm is propped up against his driver-side window, holding his head up as his fingers grip the hair on the top of his head. He looks so defeated it makes my heart hurt.

"How's your mom?" I ask, sitting up in my seat and wiping the sleep from my face.

"She's alive," he croaks, not giving me anything more.

"And you?" I ask, my eyebrow raising as I look him over.

He tilts his head toward me, pulling his lips up in a lopsided smile. "Better now."

I press my lips together as a blush spreads up my cheeks.

He swaps hands with the steering wheel and reaches for my hand in my lap. His large palm swallows my hand in his as he brings it up to his lips and presses a warm kiss to the backs of my fingers. My body burns at the feel of his soft lips on my skin, and I swallow down the thick lump of desire in my throat.

"Are you okay to drive home?"

"Or you can take me home with you." My words are out before my brain has even had time to process what the fuck just came out. "If you don't want to be alone right now, that is." I don't want to leave his side.

Chase releases a heavy sigh and shakes his head. "I don't want to be alone anymore, Izzy," he says, squeezing my hand in his.

"Then I'm not going anywhere."

I run my other hand up his arm. "So, what happened?" I ask, trying hard not to focus on his thumb now tracing circles against my knee.

His hand stills before he lets out another deep, heavy sigh, and I instantly regret asking.

"You don't have to talk about it if you don't want to. I'm here regardless, Chase." I trail my fingers over his knuckles.

"Thank you. You being here and sticking with me really means more to me than you could know." He squeezes my knee and returns to tracing circles before he continues. "So, Nora, whom I had already locked in her bedroom before I left to see you tonight, busted out and stole my neighbor's car, and then proceeded to crash into a parked police cruiser. Also, she never told me about the liver disease diagnosis she got last year."

"Chase." My voice is thick with emotion. "That's fucked up. I'm so sorry."

He maneuvers the car into a spot and removes his hand from mine before slamming the shifter into park. The streetlight he parks under illuminates his face, giving me a front-row seat to the stress, anger, and desperation he has been drowning in for so long.

"She's going to jail this time, and I can't do anything to help her," his voice cracks as he drops his head back onto the headrest and squeezes his eyes shut. "I don't want to fucking help her. I'm done. I'm so done it's eating me up inside. This emptiness inside of me when I think of her...I can't stand it." I jump in my seat as he throws his fist out and punches my steering wheel. Poor Betty is used to the abuse. "And do you want to know the worst part?" he asks, his face crumbling before he shoves the emotion away and continues. "For a minute there, I really thought she was dead, and I fucking reveled in those sixty goddamn seconds. Just sweet fucking relief at the thought of finally not having to worry about her. God, what is wrong with me to think like that?! Feel like this for my own mother?!" He wraps his arms over his face, and my heart jumps into action. I climb over the center console and squeeze into Chase's lap. He drops his arms and stares at me in confusion as his hands grip my waist.

"Izzy, what are you—" I cut him off and place the palms of my hands around his strong jaw, forcing him to see only me and what I see when I look at him.

"There isn't a thing wrong with you, Chase. I can't speak for your mother or her demons, but you and your beautiful heart are the rarest stone set in imperfection and still you shine. Still, you make the world a better place, my world a better place, simply because you are."

Chase stares at me for what feels like an eternity. The pain in his eyes melts away right before my eyes.

"Where have you been all my life, Izzy?"

The look in his eyes sets my skin ablaze. My heart is beating so loud in my chest I know he has to hear it, feel it. "I think I've been waiting for *you*," I confess.

His thumb reaches up and pulls my bottom lip free before his lips are on mine, pressing a soft kiss against them.

"Let's get inside," he says, turning the car off.

I nod my head and begin climbing back over the center console before Chase pulls me back and swings his driver-side door open.

I wrap myself around him as he climbs out, holding me up easily in his strong arms. He slides my body down against his until my feet hit the ground, and he wraps his hand over mine, kicking the door shut behind him. I follow him up a stone path and neatly manicured patch of grass and onto a small front porch.

He unlocks the door and swings it open, letting me walk in first, but before I can take in my surroundings, I'm spun around and lifted up into his strong arms. He kicks the door shut and crashes his mouth onto mine as I wrap myself around him. His heavy footsteps echo around us as he blindly moves us through his home. I'd be lying if I said I haven't spent a few or more nights imagining where he lived, but right now, there is no way I am capable of pulling away from his lips to find out.

Up a flight of stairs and a few more steps, my back collides with a door. Chase presses his body against mine, pulling his mouth back from mine an inch. His warm breath brushes against my lips as we catch our breath.

"You don't know how bad I've wanted you," he mutters against my lips. My body arches in response to his words. To be wanted for the first time in so long. His lips trail down the curve of my neck, burning my skin with his touch.

"Chase," I gasp, his name escaping my lips in a mixture of need and utter desire. My sex clenches as he groans in response, and the deep, primal sound vibrates against my heated skin, sending a shiver down my spine.

His forehead meets mine as his hands slip under my shorts and glide up and down my thighs, the sensation searing through me and the fabric separating us.

"I want you—hell, I need you right now, but I can wait. If this is too fast, we can stop right now. I'll go to bed on the couch downstairs, and you can have my bed—"

"Fuck that." I thread my fingers through his hair, pulling his mouth back down to mine. This kiss turns into something frantic and desperate. The intensity of it threatens to obliterate the one before. Hell, his mouth alone is capable of destroying me, and being destroyed by this man is exactly what I want—or even more than that right now, it might be what we both need.

14

CHASE

This is definitely the worst time to be starting this with Izzy, but there is no way in hell I'm going to stop now.

With one hand still wrapped around Izzy's waist, I hold her tight against me and swing open my bedroom door. Without removing our lips from each other, I continue to guide us blindly through my room until I feel the foot of my bed at my legs. One hand moves to the side of her neck, deepening an already intense kiss. Her heart pulsates a rapid rhythm against my thumb as my cock strains painfully behind the fabric of my shorts.

Lowering myself onto the bed, I gently lay Izzy down, letting my lips trail down her body. My fingertips push up her t-shirt, and I press my lips onto the soft skin of her stomach. She sucks in a breath as I place another one higher and higher until I'm pulling the fabric over her sports bra. The crisscross design of the front hugs her breasts and makes my goddamn mouth water. I drop down and latch onto a breast, biting at the padding in my way.

"Take this off," I damn near beg as I pull her t-shirt up over her head.

Izzy lifts up onto her elbows and tugs on the fabric, pulling it off and dropping it over the edge of my bed. I tear my shirt off and immediately drop my head down in between her breasts, grabbing them in my hands, massaging and twisting the tips of her peaked nipples. I work my tongue over the curves of each breast and take a nipple in my mouth, licking, sucking, and scraping my teeth against her sensitive skin. Izzy wraps her arms around my head, squirming beneath me.

I lean up onto an elbow, watching with hooded eyes as I slip my hands between us and let my fingers trail across her waistband. Her hands shoot up to cover her stomach. I shake my head, most definitely offended.

"Don't hide from me, Izzy. Ever." I move her hands over her head and grip them with one hand as the other skates down her stomach. "I want to see you." I gaze down at her as my hand slips under her shorts and underwear. "Every single inch of you," I say as I slide two fingers inside of her and take her mouth into mine, swallowing the moan that escapes her.

I slowly work my fingers in and out of her, watching with fascination as her hips move against me.

"That's it, baby. Ride my hand like you're going to ride my cock."

"Yes." Her breath quickens as she chases her release. I can't take my eyes off her, watching as she fucks my hand. She's so close I can feel her tightening around my fingers, but I can't wait another second without tasting her.

I remove my hand, and Izzy cries out.

"No, no, no," she begs as I slide down between her legs and latch onto her wet pussy.

"Oh," she cries out while I suck and lick over her swollen clit until her fingers are grasping my hair as she shatters before me.

I lean back up, hovering over her, my gaze fixed on her. Cheeks flushed and lips slightly parted, her eyes look up at me. Time seems to stand still as it hits me like a ton of bricks how bad I want this with her.

"I hope you know I'm not done with you yet," I say, pressing a kiss to her chin, then her lips.

"Hmm, well you're the one with your shorts still on."

"That can be fixed," I say to her as I jump out of my bed. I open my nightstand and grab a condom, then swiftly drop my shorts. Izzy sits up on her side, and her gaze locks onto my cock.

I tear open the condom and drag it down over my length, slowly stroking it a few times as my eyes ravage her naked body.

"You're so beautiful," I say as I lean back over her and settle myself between her thick thighs. Fuck, I want to live right here and never leave.

"So are you," she says, her eyes fluttering closed as I press myself right up against her. Her fingers rake over my back. Her touch sends a shiver down my spine.

"Fuck me, Thor," she breathes, biting down on her bottom lip and hitching her thighs over my hips. She draws me in closer, but I pull back just as the head of my cock teases her.

"As flattering as being compared to the Norse god is, baby, the only name I want to hear you screaming is mine." I grab onto her hips and slide myself all the way into her. So tight, so wet, so fucking perfect.

The palm of Izzy's hand shoots out as a whimper falls from her lips. I stop moving and give her body a moment to adjust to all of me.

I lean down and trace around a hard nipple before taking it into my mouth. I pull out and push myself back in as Izzy moans above me.

Her hands glide down my chest, to my backside, pulling me down.

My mouth meets Izzy's blindly, swallowing her soft moans. I pull out and thrust in again and again.

"Chase."

"Fuck," I groan, knowing fucking well I am not going to last long with the addictive rhythm of her hips meeting my every thrust.

I wrap my arms around her and flip us over, keeping my cock still happily buried inside of her.

"Take it," I tell her, moving her hands and placing them on my chest. She rolls her seductive hips over me.

"Take whatever you need, baby."

She grinds herself against me, rocking into me and throwing her head back.

"That's it." I sit up, my cock twitching inside of her as her muscles pulsate around me, squeezing me tight.

"I'm going to come!" she cries out.

I bring both of my hands down to her hips and pound relentlessly into her, skin slapping against skin until her orgasm erupts through her, taking me right down with her. I suck in a breath as the intensity of my own release holds me fucking prisoner while it tears out of me.

Izzy tumbles forward, her head resting in the crook of my neck. I can feel her heart pounding against me, matching my own as we both try to catch our breath.

"Holy fucking hell. That really happened, right?" she whispers. I can feel her lips smiling against my neck.

My hand glides up her spine, fingers tracing the curve of her back until they reach her neck. I grasp a handful of her hair and tug slightly back. With a smile still on her lips, she locks her eyes on mine.

"This feels pretty real to me, but just in case..." I whisper and wrap my arms around her back, pulling her down with me onto the bed, "let's not leave this room."

She leans up on my chest, amused. "Only," she begins, pointing a finger at me, "if you promise this is the only cardio you'll be making me do from now on."

"Oh, I promise you, this is most definitely getting added to the workout plan."

She laughs softly and shakes her head, covering her face with the palms of her hands before burying her face in my chest.

Then she pops her head up. "Please tell me the gym doesn't have anything prohibiting client-trainer relations or anything like that, because I will quit my membership right the fuck now."

Everything inside of me stills. Her words feel like a bucket of ice-cold water over me.

"Oh no, there is!" she laughs out. I try to clear the lump lodged in my throat and think of the right words to say. "It's all good. I don't need a gym membership when I've got you," she says so fucking sweet it makes my stomach twist.

"I don't know if the gym has rules like that, but if it did, this kind of makes it all work out for us, anyway." I stumble through my words like an idiot. "Izzy, I'm not actually a trainer—at all."

She smiles, clearly confused as her brows pinch together. "That doesn't make any sense."

"I don't work at the gym." I reach my hand out to touch her, but she jerks back.

"But you've been training me." Her eyes narrow into small slits.

"Izzy—" I start before she cuts me off.

"You've been lying to me?" she says, leaning back up and away from my touch. She stands up and searches the floor for her clothes.

"Why? Who even does that, Chase?" I try to stand, but she stops me with a hand in the air. Her voice rises as she continues to get more upset. "Who lies about being a personal trainer, then goes out of their way to fucking train a random-ass person?"

"You're not some random person, Iz." I rub the palm of my hand over my face, wishing like hell we could just go back to where we were a few minutes ago. "Look, when we first met, you assumed I worked there, and then you assumed I was a personal trainer, and I just didn't correct you. And I was going to tell you, but then Damon started running his mouth and—"

"Is this some game you two play to pick up women?"

"What? No. What are you talking about?" I stand and take a step toward her, my heart sinking as she takes a step back away from me.

The condom is still wrapped around my cock, so I pull it off and tie it at the end. "Let me take care of this, and then I'll explain," I say, hoping I can figure out the right thing to say to make this right.

She doesn't respond, but the hurt in her eyes is so fucking evident I have to look away, knowing I'm the one who put it there.

I quickly exit my bedroom and stomp over to my bathroom, before rushing back to Izzy. As I reenter the room, she's fully dressed and is putting her sneakers on.

"You're leaving?" I ask, desperately wishing she'd give me a chance.

"It's late. I have an early morning," she replies without even looking up at me.

"You aren't even going to let me explain? You're acting as if I—"

"I'm acting as if you lied to me, Chase, because that's what you did—*have* been doing every single day for weeks." Her voice is filled with disappointment.

"Izzy," I plead, reaching for her again.

"God, you're all the same!" She pushes past me, her footsteps carrying down the stairs until she slams the front door behind her.

"Fuuuck!" I snatch my shorts off the floor and put them on. Grabbing my phone, I rush down after her. Her car is still parked in front of my house. I glance down the dark street toward the few blocks that separate her house from mine. My bare feet pound down the unforgiving sidewalk as I call her phone, hoping I'll at least hear it nearby, but it goes straight to her voicemail.

"Izzy, call me, please."

I try her again and again as I run down the few blocks to her house. There's no sign of her anywhere. Even if she had made it all the way home, I would have seen her ahead of me. It's as if she just disappeared.

"What the fuck!" I mutter to myself, shoving my hand into my hair in frustration.

My phone buzzes with a new message.

Isadorrra: I'm fine, Chase. Go home.

Me: You shouldn't have walked all this way alone, Izzy.

Isadorrra: I didn't.

Me: Can we please just talk?

Isadorrra: Tomorrow. I'm exhausted.

Me: Technically it already is tomorrow.

She doesn't reply. I stare at her front door a second longer before tucking my hands into my front pockets and trudging back up the street. It's then that I notice the cool night air against my bare chest.

My stomach drops at the empty space where Izzy's car was parked earlier. I walk back into my house and slam the door shut behind me. Izzy's scent is everywhere. It hangs in the air, up the stairs, and damn near suffocates me when I land back into my bed.

I wake up to my phone ringing and jump up out of bed, answering it without even looking.

"Izzy?"

"Pumpkin?" Everything inside of me freezes at the sound of Nora's voice on the other side of the phone.

"Pumpkin, are you there, baby? It's Mama."

"I'm here," I push the words out of my mouth as my throat tightens. I can't remember the last time she was sober enough to call me by that moniker.

"Oh, it's so good to hear your voice. I've missed you. I want to come home, pumpkin. Will you come get me?"

"Mom," my voice cracks. "Nora, you're sick. You need help."

"I know. I know. But not here. Not like this. Please, I just want to come home, pumpkin."

I've heard this song a thousand times, and as old as it gets, it doesn't ease the ache in my chest at the sound of her voice. It makes the loneliness in this house echo off the walls.

"Pumpkin, please, you need to come and get me."

"I'll be there later."

"No, I need you now!"

A second voice sounds on her side of the phone. "Miss Nora, what are you— Don't pull those out!"

"Mom, just let them do their job. Calm down. Please," I cry out, threading my hands through my hair as I listen helplessly to Nora screaming for help on the other side of the line. The call disconnects.

I know she wasn't calling for me. It's not me she needs. It never has been.

I lower the phone in my hand between my legs and stare at the screen as it jerks in my trembling hands, my last message to Izzy staring me in my face. *For once I just wanted one thing for myself.*

My breaths come fast as my chest pounds in my ears. I rear back, throwing my phone across the room, but it does nothing to relieve the searing pressure inside of me.

15

IZZY

"G-Ma, she's still on the couch. We want to play!" Adolfo's annoying, high-pitched voice rips me from my sleep, followed by stomping, which I can bet is my mother's.

"*Carajo,* not again! Isadora Leticia Peña Yotún De La Vega, get your ass up." I groan and turn over on the sofa, careful not to fall off, and cover my head with my pillow.

"Come on, come on. Papi Thor should be here any minute," she says, swiping the blanket off me. I quickly sit up and tug the piece of fabric back from her hands a little too forcefully, causing her to stagger back slightly. Her head jerks back, and her eyebrows shoot so far up her forehead they touch her hairline. I can practically see the *Who the fuck do you think you are?* flashing in her mind right now. And if I wasn't a grown-ass woman, I would be scared as hell, expecting a full-on ass whooping. Who am I kidding? She could reach for the *chancleta* on her foot and still whoop my ass with it. I'm just so sick and tired of everything right now.

"He's old enough to be your son, Lordes, not your daddy, and he's not coming," I mutter, burying myself back under the covers. My heart sinks at the thought of Chase. How was it just a few hours ago that he was bringing me to ecstasy?

"Old enough to be my son, my ass." I feel her sit down on the edge of the couch behind me. "I'm going to ignore your momentary slip, because clearly something has happened," she says, rubbing my arm.

"Aw, shit, I knew I didn't trust his pretty ass. What did he do?" Leslie calls out from the kitchen. Her footsteps are followed by the savory scent of empanada wafting in the air. It penetrates my senses, even through the blanket over my face, and all I see is Chase and the way his eyes lit up when he took his first bite of doughy, meat-filled goodness.

Ugh, now he's ruined empanadas for me, damnit.

Unbidden tears fall down my face, and I have to cover my mouth to silence my cries.

"*Ay, mami,* what happened?" Mom pleads.

"Nothing. It doesn't matter." I sniffle, wiping at my cheeks as I sit up. "He's a liar, and I should have known better by now than to let him in. What is wrong with me that I'm so oblivious to a man's bullshit?"

"Pretty sure it's hereditary," Leslie mutters under her breath, nodding her head at Mom. Mom shoots her a piercing glare before redirecting her attention back to me.

"Before you start blaming me for your relationship woes, tell me what happened," she says, her tone soft.

"He's a liar, just like Esteban, just like my dad and all the other men that have come into my life. He's been lying to me from the moment we met. He isn't a personal trainer. He doesn't even work at the gym."

"Why?" they both ask simultaneously. I shrug my shoulders, racking my brain for any plausible answer other than the only one I've come up with.

"He probably does this all the time. Offers free training to helpless women like me just so he can get in between their legs," I grumble, crossing my arms in frustration. My cheeks burn with the thought of how damn easily I opened my legs and wrapped them around him.

"Ooooh, *sucia*! You climbed his mountain! You let him all up in there. Details, girl!" Leslie exclaims.

"*Callate, muchacha*. Now is not the time," Ma says, shaking her head, but I catch her mouthing the word "*later*" to Leslie who nods in agreement. "Izzy, I want you to take a moment and think about this, okay? Because I think you're not seeing the whole picture here. Does Chase really seem like the kind of person to stoop that low and do something like that? And for what? Just to get laid?"

"Why are you taking his side?" I ask defensively.

"Oh, no. I'm team Peña all day, mami. You know that. I just don't want you tormenting yourself like you did something wrong here."

"I'm sorry, but no. I don't see it," Layla cuts in out of nowhere, walking in and shaking her head. "Hear me out." She takes a seat on the coffee table in front of us. "You meet a fine-ass guy—"

"Hey!" Mom gives her a warning look.

"My bad, my bad. Hella-hot, gorgeous specimen of a man at the gym who dotes on you when your clumsy ass—"

"Nena," Mom's voice raises in another warning.

"Sorry, sorry, but she is clumsy. So, whatever, you fall over your two left feet, and this guy then offers to help you work out so you don't kill yourself because..." She pauses and motions over me with her hand. "And then, he goes out of his way for five or six days out of the week, practically taking on a whole extra job you're telling me he's not getting paid for. And let's not forget the time he's been spending here hanging out, *not* working out, and just chillin' with us, getting to know your family and, most importantly, *you*," Layla finishes, pointing at me.

"That is one mighty long game to be playing just for some *na-na*." Leslie whistles, nodding her head in agreement.

Suddenly, the three of them erupt into loud, cackling laughter. Leslie falls to her knees, clutching her stomach with one hand.

"It's not that funny," I mutter under my breath, mulling over the very valid facts I'd chosen to ignore.

Mom fans her face beside me, trying to dry the tears threatening to ruin her makeup. "What am I going to do with you girls?" she breathes out, finally regaining her composure.

"But what did Chase have to say?" Lydia chimes in from behind us. I roll my eyes and turn around to see her, along with Liam, Alfonso, and Aiden, sitting at the bottom of the stairs.

"How has this turned into a family discussion?" I huff, tossing my head back into the couch.

"More like an intervention," Leslie responds. "You're being extra as hell for a guy who is crazy about you, and you can't even see it."

"I thought you didn't trust him."

"I don't trust anybody."

"True." Layla nods in agreement.

"I didn't stay long enough to find out his reasoning. I just needed space to process everything."

"Izzy, he's not Esteban," Mom says.

"Esteban didn't lie to get with me. He just lied about promising forever." I groan. "And why are you pressing me about this like you haven't kicked good men to the curb for things smaller than lies?"

"I'm pressing you," she says, "because you don't know anything about the relationships or those good men you claim I kicked to the curb, okay? I love, love. The burn, the risk, the vulnerability, and the excitement of something new that could possibly change you for the better in ways you never knew you needed. Unfortunately, sometimes, none of that lasts, but that doesn't mean you give up and make your heart a forbidden place."

"You were never happy with Esteban, Izzy, but Chase...he lights you up from the inside out. You deserve more of that. Don't sacrifice that happiness now that you have found it because...what? You're scared? You are stronger than you know, but I promise you if you fall, I will be right there to catch you."

"Me too," Layla says, sitting down next to me and wrapping an arm around my other shoulder.

"Me three!" Lydia wraps her arms behind me.

"And us." The boys all run over, Liam jumping into my lap.

"And even me," Leslie says, smooshing the top of my head with the palm of her hand.

"Fine, okay. I like him. A lot. Like, I think I'm falling for him hard, but that's insane. It's too much too soon for me to be feeling like this."

"You can be in a relationship for years and feel nothing, or you can be in one for a few weeks and feel everything. It's not about the time put into it but the connection."

The doorbells rings, interrupting us, and we all freeze, probably wondering who it could be.

Mom raises an eyebrow as she stands from her seat.

"Maybe it's Chase," Liam says, running over to the door and swinging it wide open.

"Esteban?" I say his name and shake my head, wondering if I am really seeing this moment.

Leslie and Layla start booing and point their thumbs down at him.

"Is there something I can help you with?" Mom asks, placing a hand on her hip.

"I just needed to talk to Izzy," he responds.

"Nobody wants you here! Get out!" Layla calls out.

I stand and cross my arms in front of myself as disappointment washes over me. Esteban is the very last person I thought it would be at the door. For a second, I thought it was going to be Chase at the door. "You haven't had anything to say to me in months, so what do you want now?" I ask as I walk over to the door beside my mom.

His eyes bounce around at everyone glaring daggers into him before he stops at me.

"Can we talk...privately?" He nods behind him.

"Anything you have to say to me, you can say in front of them."

"Izzy, come on."

"No," I respond firmly.

"I have things to do, Esteban, so what do you want?"

"Are you okay? You look like you've been crying."

I burst into laughter. "Are you serious right now?" I say.

"I know. You're right. I'm sorry, okay? I'm sorry about everything. I—"

"Okay, you're seven months too late, E. And you know what? I don't fucking forgive you. You strung me along for years for what? Until someone better came along? Fuck you."

"Yeah, forget you, Esteban!" everyone chimes in behind me.

"Now excuse me, I have somewhere I need to be," I say as I shove my feet into my sneakers.

"Izzy, we should have had this talk a long time ago. I'm not asking for much, fuck, just a few minutes." He pleads but his annoyance slips through. This isn't about me but him stoking his own ego right now.

I dart into the entryway closet beside me and grab a sweater when I spot the one I took from him and pick it up and toss it to him.

"And you can have this back. I wasted four years on you, Esteban. I'm not wasting another second on you now. So, no, I will not give you a minute of my time."

Applause breaks out behind me as everyone claps. "Finally!" Leslie cheers.

"Bye, hope to never see you again," Layla chimes.

"Go get your man, Izzy!" my mom calls as I dash down the stairs.

16

CHASE

I stare down at the phone in my hands, my fingers hovering over the screen as I struggle to find the right words to type out to Izzy. What could I possibly say to her right now to make this right? Not a single thing comes to mind as I sit in the hospital room with Nora.

I've been here since her call this morning. They had to give her Ativan to calm her down earlier, but since then, she awoke like a completely different person. She's sitting up in bed, smiling, and even complying with all the nurses' requests.

It makes my stomach twist into knots as she plays pretend when I could be at Izzy's right now. I glance up at her as she finger-combs the tangles in her dull blonde hair. I can only wonder how much more of this I can take before the hollow pit in my stomach swallows me whole. I feel nothing but indifference for this woman, and for the first time in my life, I don't feel bad or guilty about it.

I don't want to be here.

She has broken something inside of me, something I wish I could fix, but I'll never be able to scratch the surface on the damage she's left on me if I don't start helping myself first and accepting the fact that I can't save my mother.

"Nora," I manage to choke out, keeping my head down and shutting my eyes. "I can't do this anymore."

"Do what, pumpkin?" she asks. Those three words sound so fucking sweet they grate against my ears like nails on a chalkboard. I force myself to look up, meeting her gaze. Her blue eyes stare back at me, and I wish so fucking much that I could see more to her than this.

"You're sick. You need help."

"You've been a good son, caring for me the way you have. I know I haven't said it enough, or ever, but thank you, pumpkin. When we get home, I promise things are going to be different. You'll see."

I shake my head instinctively at her words, my body tensing and heart pounding in my chest as my brain replays time after time where the bit of hope those words used to give me were torn to shreds a moment later.

"It won't, and I can't keep living like this. I can't keep choosing you."

"What's that supposed to mean? What, you're just going to walk out now that I'm sick and need you?"

"When haven't you needed me, Ma? Who else is going to pay your bar tabs, bail you out of jail, pay your medical bills and the goddamn lawyer fees? Do you know how much debt I'm in because of you?"

She shakes her head. "I'm your mother."

A chuckle escapes me at that. "You damn sure haven't ever acted like it, Nora." I stand to my feet.

"You ungrateful bastard!" she screams. "I should have known you'd abandon me just like your father."

"Well, I wish I was more like him!" I shout back. "Maybe then I wouldn't have wasted my entire life chasing you around town! You need fucking help, Nora!"

"I don't need anything, especially from you!" She hurls the bed table in front of her in my direction. I catch it before it slams into me, the cup of ice on it spilling out. A nurse opens the door.

"Is everything okay in here?" she questions, a single eyebrow arched as her gaze cautiously bounces between us.

"I want him gone!" Nora says, pointing at me. "Get him out of here!" Nora shouts.

"Sir?" The nurse gestures toward the door.

"Okay," I say, nodding my head. "Good luck to you, Nora." I turn and brush past the nurse, slamming the door shut behind me.

"Keagan, wait," I hear her call me back, and for the first time ever, I don't turn around. I don't succumb to the guilt that gnaws at me when she calls. I push forward and barrel down the hallway. It isn't until I'm walking out of the lobby that I release the heaviness that's been building inside me. A warm breeze sweeps by, carrying it away, and I breathe in through my nose. I get a surprising lungful of an intoxicatingly sweet scent that reminds me of Izzy. I shake my head at my delirious mind for conjuring her perfume and scrub the palms of my hands over my face.

"Chase?"

I spin around at the sound of her voice. I expect it to be a figment of my imagination, but she's here, in front of me. Another soft breeze sweeps by, pushing dark strands of hair into her face. My fingers immediately move to push them back, while my heart lodges itself in my throat.

"Izzy." It's only been hours, but it feels like so much more time has passed between us since she was in my arms.

"What are you doing here?" I ask, tucking my hands into my front pockets to keep from reaching out and touching her.

"I came to bring you these." She waves a white pastry box in front of her as she slowly approaches me.

"You brought me food?" I narrow my eyes at the box in confusion.

"Technically, they're from Lulu."

Her words hang in the air.

I stare at her, searching her eyes for more than just her showing up to deliver food.

"Can we talk?" we both blurt out in unison.

I raise my hand in the air between us. "I just need you to know…" I begin, my eyebrows pulling together as she nervously bites her bottom lip. I hold her gaze, stepping closer to her. "I could never intentionally hurt you, Izzy." My hand reaches out, gently brushing her hair away from her face. "You thinking that I'm that level of douche makes me sick to my stomach. I'm sorr—"

Before I can finish my sentence, she interrupts me, pressing a finger to my lips.

"I know exactly the kind of man you are," she declares. I can't breathe as her eyes hold mine, and her finger traces a path down my lips, chin, and then glides over my racing heart. She opens her hand and presses it against my chest. I breathe out slowly and lean into her touch, needing her so much more than she could ever know. "You're a good man. Thoughtful, selfless, always putting others first. You're loyal and kind beyond measure, and your heart...it's the sweetest, most generous one I have ever known." She takes a step closer, closing the distance between us. "You are the kind of man that is deserving of all the love this world has to give." The sound of my heart pounding in my chest echoes with her words. No one in all my life has spoken words like those to me. I'm fucking speechless, not knowing how to respond.

"I'm sorry for how I reacted earlier," she continues. "I should have heard you out."

Shaking my head, I reach out to brush my thumb along the soft skin of her cheek. "You have nothing to apologize for." Relief washes over me when her face leans into my touch. "You deserve all of that too, you know?" I lift her chin. "To be cherished, appreciated, and loved. If you'll let me, I want to be the one to give you that, Izzy."

She looks up at me, her eyes shining bright and her lips curving into a soft smile.

"I want that too," she whispers, and my heart soars in my chest. Without hesitation, I lean down and capture her lips with mine, wrapping my arms around her.

The box in her hands falls to the ground. I pull back and press my forehead against hers, our breaths mingling. "Come home with me?" I ask.

Izzy pulls her bottom lip between her teeth again as she nods her head.

"Wait, how's your mom doing?" she asks, concerned.

"Better. I think this time around is going to be different for her."

"That's great, Chase. I really hope that for her."

Waking up to Izzy's terrible singing on a Sunday morning is one of my new top favorite ways to start the day, her offbeat voice filling the air and replacing the arrant silence that usually wakes me. The sight of her naked in my bed and the first thing I see in the morning is my number one favorite. I can't help smiling to myself as I stretch my arms out, the memory of yesterday still fresh in my mind. This is real. She's here and all fucking mine.

Grabbing a condom from my nightstand, I walk out into the hallway, not bothering with putting clothes back on since I'm planning on joining Izzy in her shower musical. She's singing in Spanish, and other than a couple words here and there, I've never really heard her speak it. The high notes she attempts to reach make me wish I understood enough so I could know what they mean.

I gently push open the bathroom door, the music from her phone on the sink muting my entrance. My eyes hungrily trace the curves of her naked silhouette behind the translucent shower curtain as her hips sway back and forth.

"*Con esos ojitos lindos. Que con eso yo estoy bien. Hoy he vuelto a nacer,*" she belts out into a shampoo bottle.

I smile to myself as I silently approach her and sneak in behind her. I glide my hands around her slick waist, startling her. She screams, dropping the shampoo bottle and jumping away from me, nearly slipping. I reach out and wrap my arms around her, pulling her against me.

"You scared the shit out of me," she says, playfully smacking me with her hand before dropping her head against my chest.

"I'm sorry," I mutter and press a kiss onto the top of her head. "I've never heard you speak Spanish before."

"Memorizing lyrics doesn't count as speaking Spanish," she says. My hands skate up and down her sides, enjoying the way she feels in my hands before cupping her breasts.

She moans, and I lean down, peppering her neck with soft kisses.

"What's the name of this song?" I ask.

"*Ojitos lindos,*" she says, spinning around and standing on her tiptoes.

"Hmm, sounds like you were speaking Spanish to me, babe."

She shakes her head and chuckles as I lean down and press a soft kiss to the side of her lips. "Oh, have we moved on to pet names already?" she asks, wrapping her arms around my neck.

"When it's my cum you're washing off of you, I'd say so... babe," I say pressing another kiss to her nose. "What's this song about?" I ask, noting it's on repeat.

"Um, about feeling different after finding love." She bites her bottom lip. I lean down and kiss her.

"I get that," I say against her mouth. I press myself against her and slide my tongue against hers, gripping her ass in my hands. I lift her up into my arms and turn us around, the water from the shower now falling over my back as I press hers against the shower wall. I revel in the feel of her thick thighs wrapping around me.

"Chase," she breathes against my lips. I slip my hand in between us and press the pads of my fingers against her clit, swallowing her gasps with my mouth as my fingers work the tight bundle of nerves. Her hips twist and turn, and I press my thick cock against her, keeping her still. Leaning down over her chest, I take a peaked tip of her dark nipple into my mouth, swirling my tongue around it in slow, languid strokes. Izzy's body trembles all around me as she chants my name like a fucking prayer.

I reach out onto the sink to get the condom and tear the wrapper open with my teeth. The head of my cock pushes into her. We both moan, reveling in this feeling, before I pull back and drive back into her again and again and again. Her cries echo off the walls until her tight pussy squeezes my cock so tight I explode with her.

Keeping her wrapped around me, I squeeze her thighs, and I rest my forehead against her shoulder. As we both try to catch our breath, she traces a slow path up and down my neck.

"I could get used to this," she whispers against my skin.

I lean back and meet her eyes. "Good," I reply, "because I'm not letting you go."

17

IZZY

ONE MONTH LATER

"Fuck me. That's the dress?" Chase's voice echoes through the twins' bedroom behind me.

I spin around as his hungry eyes trail down my body. Thank God for my mother's sense of style. The bridesmaid dress she picked out fits perfectly. A soft-pink, sheath-style, satin gown with a deep side slit and crisscrossed back. The low-cut neckline is snug and securely holds my breasts before cinching in at my waist and subtly draping over my curves, hugging them in all the right places.

My hand falls to my stomach, a weak attempt at settling the butterflies that have still not gotten used to the heated look in his eyes.

I know I look good right now. Honestly, it is the best I have looked in a very long time, and the few pounds I've lost these few months surprisingly are not the reason why.

"You're perfect, you know that?" Chase's deep voice ripples through me as he stalks toward me, slipping his hand in the slit of my dress, his fingers trailing up my upper thigh. I bite my bottom lip, waiting for the moment he realizes I'm not wearing anything else.

How could I ever feel anything less than perfect when he makes me feel like a carved piece of stone?

"Are you trying to kill me?" he groans, dropping his forehead to mine.

"I have no idea what you're talking about," I reply innocently, peering up at him.

My hands slide along the length of his crisp white dress shirt. I am not at all surprised at how well he cleans up. My hands wrap around his shoulders, missing the feel of my fingers curling around the ends of his hair. I run them over the top of his newly buzzed hair instead.

The change looks good on him, but it is still taking me some time to get used to.

His hand wraps around my hip, pulling me to him. He leans down to kiss me, but I take a step back before things escalate and I scar one of my siblings with a peep show.

"Don't you dare try to start something you won't be able to finish," I say, pressing my hand against his hard chest.

"Who says I won't be able to finish?" he replies, pushing against the little restraint I have.

"Eww! Please go and get any other room that isn't mine." Layla bursts in with a hand over eyes peeking through her fingers.

Chase hides behind me, pulling me back against him and his growing length.

"We were just leaving. Is everyone else ready?" I ask as she leans over her bed, pulling her phone charger out of its outlet.

While Mom, Leslie, and Lydia are at the venue, putting the finishing touches on everything, I stayed back to drive everyone else there.

"Yup, just needed to grab my charger. You guys didn't do anything nasty in here, right? This is my sanctuary, and I would never forgive you."

"Of course not, Lay. Scout's honor," Chase says.

"Thor, please, you were not in no Boy Scouts." She scoffs.

"You know we wouldn't do something like that. Besides..." I turn around in Chase's arms and roam my hands over his chest. "I have my own apartment now, where I get to have my way with Thor without any interruption from any of my annoying siblings."

"Eww, stop talking." She turns and walks out.

"You started it," I call out after her. "What?" I ask as Chase eyes me. "She did. Besides, I knew physical touch would get rid of her."

"Mm-hmm, you need to stop touching me like that, then, or we won't make it home," he cautions, pulling me into him.

Home, he says.

It makes my heart pound a little harder in my chest at the gravity of that one word. How he could mean so much to me in just a few months.

"Oh, that reminds me, I have something for you."

I walk around him to my purse and rummage through it until my fingers make contact with the small leather box.

Doubt whispers in my head, but I push it down, focusing instead on what is true, what is real.

I hand him the small box, realizing suddenly how much it looks like a wedding ring box.

What if he thinks—

"It's not what you think," I immediately correct. "It's just— I thought— I mean, you've spent almost every night with me anyway, and I just thought this would make it easier."

Chase eyes the box in my hand curiously before popping it open. A smile twitches at the corners of his mouth as he takes the key out.

"I almost thought..." He chuckles softly, more to himself, I think.

"That'd be crazy," I respond, suddenly feeling dumb.

"It's only been a few months."

"And that would definitely be jumping the gun. We haven't even said 'I love you' yet," I say, forcing a laugh. Chase stands quietly, staring at the key in his hand.

Maybe it was too much too soon. My cheeks burn in embarrassment, and I wish I could just reach out and throw the key back in my bag so we can go back to where we were.

"But I do. You know that, right?" His gaze locks on mine, a serious look taking over.

"What?"

"I— Shit. I haven't said it out loud, but I do...love you."

My heart stops in my chest as he continues.

"I've been free-falling for you since you landed in my arms, Izzy. And every day since has only been better than the last. I'm in love with every single thing about you, even the parts you want to change, because to me, you are perfect, Izzy."

He takes a step forward.

"Chase, I—"

"You don't have to say it back. I mean, you're right. It is crazy. But I am crazy about you," he says, his hand reaching over and tracing my bottom lip.

"I love you too," I let out, and his touch stills.

"You do?" he says after a beat.

"Of course I do."

"Say it again." His fingers curl around the nape of my neck as he pulls me into him.

"I love you," I breathe against his mouth.

"Are you serious right now? You guys can literally do this whenever you want. Come on," Layla groans in the background, but all I hear are his next four words.

"I love you, Isadora," he says against my lips before catching my mouth in his.

TO BE CONTINUED IN...

ACKNOWLEDGMENTS

First and foremost, I just want to thank each and every one of **you** for taking a chance on me and reading my debut Novella. This journey hasn't been easy, but through perseverance, sweat and literal tears we finally made it!

Thank you to my family, for putting up with me and supporting me as I neglected, the house, the dishes and sometimes even them. Josue, I wouldn't have gotten here without you, my love. Thank you for absolutely everything.

My mom, brothers and sister-in-laws for being the very first to pre-order and be nothing but supportive of me.

To my niece, Jessica, who read the original story and beta read this one, thank you for sharing how seen and connected you felt to my Izzy. This is for you, boo and for more stories that represent us.

To my BABWKA's, Andrea and Natasha Monique, for your unwavering support in me and constantly getting me out of my own head. You have been there to lift me up, share in my highs and lows, and inspire me to keep pushing forward. We some badass bitches who kick ass and I am forever grateful for you girls.

To my *Comay*, who has read every single version of this story and loved them all. Thank you for believing in me and loving my words even on the days I couldn't. For devoting so much of your own time and energy to brainstorm with me and read everything I sent your way.

Anna Lindgren, I freaking love you. Thank you for always checking in on me, for your support through all of these years and always your honest and helpful feedback. I appreciate you so much!

To Jenn Lockwood for coming through last minute and getting edits done just in time.

To the writing community, who inspire me every day to pursue this wild dream of mine. Your encouragement and support means the world to me.

To the countless others who have played a part in my writing journey, thank you from the bottom of my heart. This novella would not have been possible without your support, belief and love.

And to you, the readers, thank you so much for taking a chance on me. This is just the beginning and I cannot wait for to share more stories with you.

ABOUT THE AUTHOR

K. Rodriguez writes sweet and spicy contemporary romance con sazón, centered on real characters, big feelings, and love that hits hard. A first-generation Dominican American author, she loves telling heartfelt stories that feel honest, familiar, and a little messy—in the best way.

Born and raised in Central New Jersey, she traded the northern winters for Southwest Florida, where she lives with her high school sweetheart, their three kids, and four spoiled fur babes.

When she isn't writing, she's homeschooling, wrangling poodles, avoiding the laundry, or blasting her old-school music playlist like it's still 2003.

Stay connected with K. Rodriguez at
www.krodromance.com
Facebook.com/krodwrites
Instagram.com/k.rodriguezwrites